Frederick A. Crisp

Collections Relating to the Family of Crispe

Vol. 3

Frederick A. Crisp

Collections Relating to the Family of Crispe
Vol. 3

ISBN/EAN: 9783337379971

Printed in Europe, USA, Canada, Australia, Japan

Cover: Foto ©Andreas Hilbeck / pixelio.de

More available books at **www.hansebooks.com**

COLLECTIONS

RELATING TO THE

Family of Crispe.

ABSTRACTS OF

WILLS AND ADMINISTRATIONS

IN THE

COURTS OF THE ARCHDEACON OF SUFFOLK,

1454—1800.

VOL. III.

1884.

CONTENTS.

Wills.

Crispe Wills.

1454.

LATIN Testament of William Cryspe of Stradbrook whole of mind &c—To be interred in the burial-ground of the parish church of Stradbrook—To the high altar of the same church for my tythes forgotten 6^d—To the light of the Blessed Mary 4^d to the sepulchre light one little veil [flameolum] and to another light 6^d—The residue of my goods to Agnes my wife John Jwrdon and William Chittyng my Ext^s and Ex^{ors} to order and dispose the same for the welfare of my soul—Latin Will of the said William Cryspe—To Agnes my wife my household goods my cows &c to her also for life my tenement and after her decease the same to be sold—Said Testament and Will dated 1 March 1453 and proved 9 April 1454.

Bk. 1, *Fo.* 116.

1459.

THE Will of John Crispe whole of mind &c dated 1 Feb 1448 was proved 21 April 1459 and Adm^{on} of his Goods &c was granted at Laxfield to Margery his wife and John Dowsing alias Smythe of Laxfield the Ext^x and Ex^{or} but only the preamble to the said Will is registered.

Bk. 1, *Fo.* 201.

1461.

LATIN Testament of John Crysp of Laxfeld—To John my son—To Johan my daughter—To Anabil my wife—Said wife and son Ext^x and Ex^{or}—Latin Will of the said John Crisp of Laxfeld " saïtere "—To said wife my tenement for life remainder to said son—Said Testament and Will dated 17 Dec 1461 and proved 25 Jan 1461-2.

Bk. 2, *Fo.* 65.

1482.

LATIN Will of William Crisp of Laxfeld in the diocese of Norwich —To be interred in the burial-ground of the church of All Saints in Laxfeld aforesaid—All my lands and tenements in Laxfeld and Stradbrook with the appurtenances to be sold—To the Vicar of Laxfeld for my burial 6ˢ 8ᵈ—To the sons of John Crisp my brother 10 marks equally between them when 21—Said brother John Crisp and John Bocher of Laxfeld Exᵒʳˢ—Dated 4 May 1482—Proved 8 July 1482.

Bk. 3, Fo. 3.

1491.

LATIN Will of John Cryspe [described in the Calendar as of Laxfield] "medicℓ" [i.e. medicus]—To be interred in the burial-ground of the church of All Saints in Laxfield—To William my son 20ˢ—To Thomas Cryspe my little son [filiolus] 12ᵈ—To Johan Petyte 8ᵈ—To Johan my daughter—John Jacob of Laxfeld and William Smyth son of Nicholas Smyth Exᵒʳˢ—Dated 4 May 1491—No Probate Act.

Bk. 3, Fo. 141.

1496.

LATIN Will of Andrew Crispe of the parish of Holy Trinity in Bungey in the diocese of Norwich—To be interred in the burial-ground of the church in the aforesaid parish—My messuage in Bungey to be sold and half of the money arising by the sale thereof to Christiana my wife—To Robert my son 5 marks out of the said money when 16 but if he dies under that age the same to remain to the church of the Holy Trinity in Bungey aforesaid—Said wife and Geoffrey Goreham Extˣ and Exᵒʳ—Robert Wyngfeld Gent. Supervisor—Witnesses Sir Robert Nicholasson Vicar of the church of the Holy Trinity aforesaid Peter Bewale Richard Fyscher and others whose names are not given—Dated 26 Oct 1496—Proved 15 Dec 1496 by the said Exˡˣ and Exᵒʳ.

Bk. 3, Fo. 194.

1504.

" I WILLM̃ CRYSPE of Holton "—" to be buryed in the cherchyerd off Saynt Petyr in Holton aforsayd "—" onto Johane my wiff my Teneme't in Laxfeld wᵗ the ptiñ " " all my household stuff & all my catell All my other goodₑ meueabyll & onmeueabyll I put them vnto the Rule off my execut õs whom I ordeyn the sayd Johane my wyff Joħ Noloth off Wynfarthyng & Aleſ peers off Holton "—Dated 24 Jan 1503—Proved 28 Sept 1504 by Johan the Relict & Alexander Peers power reserved to John Noloth.

Bk. 4, Fo. 151.

4

" I ALYS KYRSPE of Wylbeye "—" to be buryed in the cherch yerde of Wylbey aforesaid "—" to eche of my children a kowe "—" to Alys my doughter iij ffarnaryngge & a bedde laufull "—" to Emme my belchild vj⁸ & viijᵈ for to be payd to her at xviij yere of age "—" to iiij of my godchildren my belchildren eche of them vj⁸ viijᵈ "—" I will that Roƀt my son do fynde a p'est to syng in the parish cherch of Wylbey by the space of halff a yere for my husbonds soule and myñ as sone as he may "—" myñ other goodes not bequeth I geve vn to Roƀt myñ son whom I make myñ executoʳ And Roƀt Harvy of Stradbrook "—Dated 7 Sept 1506—Proved 14 Dec 1506 by Robert Kyrspe Robert Harvy the other Exᵒʳ having renounced.

Bk. 5, *Fo.* 1.

" I ROBT KYRSPE of Laxfeld "—" to be buryed in the cherche yerde of Laxfeld aforesaid "—" I geue to a p'est to syng iij messes at Rome for my ffather & my mother and for me vj⁸ viijᵈ "—" vn to John my son my Teñt callyd Kryspes lyeng in Laxfeld and Denyngton "—" I will that my teñt at the cherch be sold "—" vn to Maryon my dowghter a ffether bedde a transü a peyer of shetys a peyer of blankettp a Coð-lyght a gyrdall & a rynge which was hir own mothers " &c—" vn to John my son a ffether bedde wᵗ all that long ther to whiche is wᵗ in hym "—" vn to Roƀt Kyrspe my godson the son of John Kyrspe my son my tawnny gowne which is at Willm̃ my sonys "—" to Thomas my son my blak gowne " " ij peyer of shetys a peyer of blankettp and ij Coð-lyghtp "—" vn to Edmunde my son vj⁸ viijᵈ "—" vn to Roƀt Kyrspe son of Thomas Kyrspe a Russett gowne "—" I will that a bras potte a panne which panne is at Willm̃ my sonys a greate Cawdren vnbownd and a gyrdyll which was my last wyffe be sold be myñ executors to fulfille this my last will "—" John Kyrspe my son and John Smyth of the Parke feld my godson " Exᵒʳˢ—Dated 1 Nov 1506—Proved 1 Dec 1506 by both the Exᵒʳˢ.

Bk. 5, *Fo.* 1.

" I JOHN CRYSPE off Becclys "—" to be buried in the cherche yerde off seynt myhell the Archangill in Becclys foreseid "—" vnto the hey Auter of the forseid Cherche for my tythes forgoten & not paid vijᵈ " " vn to the holy Gost Gylde in Becclys oon dishe & oon plater off pewter "—" vn to the gilde off seynt myhell in Beccles I giff & bequeth my Tenement lyeng in Northgate strete late of John Chyrcheman "—" my vtensybill off howsehold I gyue & bequeth vnto the disposiçon off Kateryn my wiff whom I ordeyn & make myñ exð "—Witnesses Sir Robert Woode & John Bronoue—Dated 9 Feb 1520—Proved 26 June 1521 by the said Extˣ.

Bk 8, *Fo.* 133.

" I WILLIAM KRYSPE of Laxfelde in the diocese of Norwich and in the Countie of Suff tanner "—" to be buried in the cherch yerde of all saynt℈ of Laxfelde beforesaid "—" I will that John my son haue my tenement and all my londes both ffre & bonde lyeng in Laxfelde" when 18 paying " to his brother Jaffrey And to eche of his susters eche of them xxvj⁸ viij ᵈ " and if the said John dies under that age then the tenement &c " to Jaffrey my son he payeng to his sisters the legacys beforesaide " but if both said sons die under 18 then the tenement and lands to be sold and my Exᵒʳˢ to find " an honest priest secular to singe for my soule and my wyffℇ soule and for all our frendys soulys by the space of ij yerys in the parish cherche of Laxfilde beforesaid " and to pay " to eche of myñ ij doughters that is to sey to Margaret myℜ doughter v ñrke " when 18 and " to Alys my doughter other v marke " when of the same age—" John Smyth my brother in lawe and Jaffrey Dallyng " Exᵒʳˢ—Witnesses " John Baas Nicholas Mason Robert ffyske And Thomas Grygℇ parish priest wᵗ other "—Dated 13 Nov 1521—Proved 14 Jan 1521-2 by both the Exᵒʳˢ.

Bk. 8, *Fo.* 217.

WILL of John Crispe of Dennington proved between these dates and registered at Fo. 268 of Book 9. Several leaves including Fo. 268 are missing from this Book and the Original Will is not extant.

" I ROB̄T CRYSPE of Laxfeld "—" to be buried in the cherch yerde of Laxfeld beforesaid "—" I will that Clemens my wiff and Herry my son shall haue and occupie together my Teñt Goodwyns till the tyme that they paye all suche dettys as I owe for the purchase of the said tenement " and then the ℮ ̄ne to said son he giving said wife yearly " durying hir lyff xiij⁸ iiijᵈ and heꝛ Ꞇhamber wᵗ sufficient ffyre wode " and paying after her decease " vnto William and John my soñys to eche of them xx⁸ " " to Elizabeth and Agnes my doughters to eche of them vj⁸ & viijᵈ " " to Symond and Gaffrey my soñys to eche of them vj⁸ viijᵈ " and " to marion my doughter and to Rob̄t my son to eche of them vj⁸ viijᵈ "—" to Clemens my wiff all my catall and my stuffe of houshold "—" to Herry my son all my barkefattys wyth the stokke "—Said wife & son " Herry " residʸ Legatees & Extˣ & Exᵒʳ—Witnesses " Jaffrey Dallyng and John Kyrspe Leche of Laxfeld "—Dated 28 July 1529—Proved 16 Aug 1529 by the said Extˣ & Exᵒʳ.

Bk. 10, *Fo.* 100.

" I THOMAS CRYSPE of Erwarton in the dioⁱ off Norwych Carpenter "—" to eche of my godsons beryng my name oon Lambe of
the next yere ffalle "—" to John Clouer oon Lambe of the next yere "—
" to Roger Jennyng of eche of my Tole ꝑte that longythe to Carpentrye
Worke "—" I will that Margarett my wiff shall haue all that myñ house
or teñt to dwell in wᵗ all the londₑ as welle Arabyll pasturs & medows
sytting & lyeng wᵗ in the Towne of Erwerton aforesaide " &c " And all
other my stuff of Houshold Cornys & Cattallₑ excepte xxⁱⁱ ₛhepe The
whych I bequeth to John my son & a mylche Cowe the whych I bequeth
to Johan Cryspe the Doughter of John Cryspe of Ippswych " and after
said wife's decease the house & lands " shall remayne to John my son &
to the heyers of hys body laufullye " [begotten] and in default of such
issue the same shall be sold—" to eche of my Doughters chyldren John &
Anne vj viijᵈ And Agnes Card my doughter xiijˢ iiijᵈ And to Margarett
Brome my doughter vjˢ viijᵈ And to Anne my doughter xxxⁱⁱ ˢ Itᵐ I
bequeth to the said Anne oon Ewe shyppe "—After said wife's decease
" all myñ aboue rehersyd stuff of Housholde Cornys & Cattallₑ shall be
solde "—" to Agnes Carde my doughter my teñt wᵗ a pece of Lond " &c
" in Erwerton aforsaide callyde Sprottₑ "—" John Cresy & John Cryspe
my son " Exᵒʳˢ—" Master Stystede off Ippeswych " Supervisor—Witnesses " Symonde Nycolas pryst Thomas Edmūde Thomas Spman &
John Clover "—Dated 31 Dec 1529—Proved 2 Dec 1535 by both the
Exᵒʳˢ.

Bk. 12, Fo. 81.

" I JAFFREY CRYSPE of Laxfelde "—" to be buryed in the Cherch
yarde of Laxfeld beforesaid "—" I will that Margarett my wyff shall
haue the occupyeng of the profyghtₑ of all my Londeₑ & Teñttₑ both free
& bonde " in Laxfield for life " wᵗ all other my moveabyllₑ & Imple-
menttₑ of Housholde "—" to Anne Kent my doughter " £20—" to
Margerye pype " £6 13ˢ 4ᵈ " wᵗ all my housholde Stuff " after the decease
of said wife and if she dies before receiving her said legacy the same
shall " be devyded evynlye amongₑ the Systern of the said Margery "—
" to Edwarde Kent son of the forsaid Anne Kent " £6 13ˢ 4ᵈ and if he
dies before receiving the amount the same shall be equally devided
" amongₑ the chyldren of the said Anne then lyuyng "—The lands &
tenements on the death of said wife " unto Thoñs Pype & Margarett his
wyff " for their lives remainder " to Jaffrey pype my Godson " & his heirs
male remʳ " to Willñ pype " & his heirs male with remʳ " to the ryght
heyers of the said Thoñs & Margaret "—" to Elyzabeth Eve aⁱs Sparhawke " 6ˢ 8ᵈ—" the said Margaret my wyff Thoñs pype & Henry
Cryspe " Extˣ & Exᵒʳˢ and the said Thomas & Henry " to haue for ther
laboʳs eche of them " 40/—Witnesses " John Stubbard thelder John
Stubbard the younger John Kent John Cryspe Tanñe John Cowp sho-
maker & Symon Cryspe the younger wᵗ other moo "—Dated 22 March
1535—Proved 26 April 1538 by Margaret the Relict & Thomas Pype
Henry Cryspe having renounced.

Bk. 13, *Fo.* 64.

" I JOHN CRYSPE of the Roake thelder of laxefylde in the cowntye of Suff and in the dyocesse of Norwyche "—"to be buryed in laxefylde churche yarde aforesayde "—"to my sonne John Cryspe the fether bedde & bolstar y⁺ I lye vpon "—"to my doughter Chrystyane I gyve my Geaste bedde w⁺ the bolster blankette " &c "and ij payer of my beaste sheetes and my brasse potte "—To "Edmonde Alrede " 6ˢ 8ᵈ but the amount to be deducted from a debt of 40/ due from him to Testator —"to frauncys Alrede my beste brasse panne and twoo pewter platters " —" All my moveable goode not before bequethyd & gyven I wyll to be devyded equally " "amonge these my chyldren in lawe followynge y⁺ ys to saye Edmonde Alrede Wyllam Kynge thelder of brundyshe Jeffry fyske my sonne in lawe Robarde Manne of ayshe & Alyce Smythe wyfe of Roger smythe of Denyngeton Except only thoblygacon of foure like sterlynge dewe to be payde by Thoms pype vpon saynte Mychaels daye nexte ensewynge after my deceasse and also xxiijˢ iiijᵈ wiche the sayde Thoms pype owe to me for the pryce of an horse " " which I putt to the disposycon of myn executors "—"Edmonde Allrede & Wyllam Kynge aforesayde " Exᵒʳˢ and " vnto eche of them I gyve iijˢ iiijᵈ "—"John Taylar of laxefylde " Supervisor to whom " vˢ for his laboure "—Witnesses "James lane bat godefrey Smythe Wyllam ferrore Edmonde Cryspe & others "—Dated 22 Nov 1544—Proved 2 March 1544-5 by both the Exᵒʳˢ.   *Original Will.*

" I WILLYAM CRISPE of Laxfelde in the countie of Suff and dyoces of Norwiche thelder turnoʳ "—" I will that Anne my wyef have and enioye to her and to her heyres and assygnes for ever all my londe and tenemente " "bothe fre and copye set lyeng and beyng in Laxfelde aforsayde "—Testator had lately purchased "of John Cryspe of Rookes" a meadow in Laxfield called "Plummes brooke "—To "Nicholas ffyske my sone in lawe " all those my messuages londe and tenemente bothe fre and copye " in "Denyngton within the saide countie of Suff" paying yearly "vnto the sayde Anne my wyef" £4 &c—"vnto Anne Noyse my doughter" £10—"to Margerie wade my doughter" £10—"to Margaret ffyske my doughter" £10—"to Johan ffyske my doughter" 5 marks—"to every of my doughters chylderne" 6ˢ 8ᵈ—"to Alyce Mayhew" 20/—"to John Mayhewe" 20/—"to John Godbalde" 6ˢ 8ᵈ—"to Margaret Cryspe" 6ˢ 8ᵈ—"to Anne Plumpton the wyef of Thomas Plumpton" £3 6ˢ 8ᵈ—"to Awdrye Mayhewe" 5 marks—"to mother Bullocke and mother Blythe" 3ˢ 4ᵈ—"to mother Pers" 12ᵈ—"to walter turnoʳ" 12ᵈ—"to Willyam Cryspe and hys howsholde" 3ˢ 4ᵈ—"to Willyam Whytman" 12ᵈ—"to father paynter" 12ᵈ—"the sayde Anne my wyef" residʸ Legatee—"Nycholas Stannerde of Laxfelde and John Noyse my sone in lawe of the same towne" Exᵒʳˢ to each of whom 15/—Witnesses "Thomas Cryspe John ffyske George Cowper Willyam ffyske John Cowper of Balstons Roger Godbalde John Hersaunte Thomas Plumpton and others "—Dated 1 Dec 1552—Proved 19 Jan 1552-3 by both the Exᵒⁱʳ.
            Bk. 16, *Fo.* 409.

1553.

" I PRYME CHRYSPE of wurlynghm̃ "—" vnto Rose my dowghter two shepe "—" vnto Robert Chrispe my soñe one amblynge mare and thre shepe "—" vnto Elysabethe Chryspe my dowghter one younge hef ker "—" vnto Añe Chryspe my dowghter one younge hef ker and thes thre children eyche of them shall haue ther forsayde gyftes delyvered them by my executryx at ther maryage dayes "—" vnto the poremenes boxe of wurlynghm̃ iiijᵈ "—" Alyce my welbeloved wyeffe " residʸ Legatee & sole Extˣ—Witnesses " Robert Pole and Robert Loue wryghter herof" —Dated 13 Oct 1553—Proved 6 Nov 1553.

Bk. 16, *Fo.* 612.

1553.

" I AÑE CRYSPE of laxfelde in the countie of Suff and diocᵱ of Norwyche "—" to be buryed within the pryshe churche yarde of Laxfelde aforsayde "—To " John Noyse my soñe in lawe " " all those my meswagᵱ londᵱ and teñtᵱ " &c held " of the manoʳ of the Rectorye in Laxfelde aforsayde " & " all that my close called Greneloves " held " of the manoʳ of Laxfelde in Laxfelde aforsayde " paying for all the said messuages &c 40 marks—" to John Godbalde the soñe of my brother Thomas Godbalde " £4 6ˢ 8ᵈ " a fether bedd in the chamber the cover-lyght vpon the same " &c—" vnto Alyce Mayhew " 5 marks when 22 to her also " a worsted kyrtle two pewter platters a candlestycke and a payer of shetᵱ "—" to Margaret Cryspe " £3 6ˢ 8ᵈ when 22—" to Añe noyse my goddowghter " £3 6ˢ 8ᵈ when 21—" to Agnes ffyske and to Hester ffyske " £3 6ˢ 8ᵈ apiece when of the same age—" to Margerye wade the dowghter of my dowghter Margerye " £3 6ˢ 8ᵈ when of the same age—" to John ffyske the soñe of my dowghter Margaret " 20/ when 24—" to everye one of the other children of my sayde dowghter margaret " 6ˢ 8ᵈ when 21—" to everye one of the children of my sayde dowghter Margerye Añe Margerye and Alyce her dowghters onlye ex-cepted " 6ˢ 8ᵈ when 21—" to wyⱡⱡm ffyske the soñe of Nycholas ffyske and Johan my dowghter " 6ˢ 8ᵈ when of the same age—" vnto Thomassyn and Martha the children of the sayde John Noyse " 20/ a piece when of the same age—To " Thomas Plumpton " " all that my meswage or teñt called Gooches " " in Laxfelde aforsayde wyth all the orchardᵱ gardyns and londᵱ bothe free and bonde therto belongynge " " vpon condicõn that Añe hys wyef haue and holde all the sayd teñte Gooches to her and to her assygnes durynge the hole terme of her naturall lyef except the sayd Thomas her husbonde do as well herafter otherwyse provyde for her " and the said Thomas to pay for the said tenement £10—" vnto Añe Noyse my dowghter my beste fether bed wyth the coverynge " &c until " Añe Noyse my goddowghter " marries and if she dies unmarried the same " to Thomasyn Noyse her syster "—" to the sayde Thomassyn Noyse my latten bason "—" to Nycholas ffyske my soñe in lawe my greateste cawdron in the fornace "—" to John Noyse my soñe in law my other cawdron "—" to Margaret ffyske my dowghter my greateste brasse pañe " & " my cupborde " but " Margaret her dowghter " to have the latter when she marries—" to John ffyske my nephye my fetherbed and the bolster that is vsed in the soller "—" to Thomas Plumpton and to

9   c

Añe his wyef two pewter dyshes vpon the cupborde two pewter dysshes in the buttrey a brasse panne" &c &c—"to John Mayhew a mattres a payer of sheetɇ and a coverynge" when 22—"to Johan ffyske my dowghter my beste mantle" & "my beste frocke"—"to Margaret ffyske my dowghter my other mantle" & "my beste gowne" —"to my dowghter Añe Noyse my gowne vnmade"—"to Añe Plumpton my purfoled gowne"—"to mother Bullocke my beste fryse frocke and a smocke"—"to mother Blythe my other fryse frocke and a smocke"—"to Añe Stannarde my goddowghter" 5/ when 24—"my fower dowghters and Añe Plumpton" residʳ Legatees—"John Noyse my sayde soñeinlawe and Nycholas ffyske my soñe in lawe" Exᵒʳˢ to each of whom 10/—Witnesses "Robert Dawlynge John Storke Robert Lane John Cowper Junior and dyvers others by me John Smythe"— Dated 23 Jan 1553—Proved 17 March 1553-4 by both the Exᵒʳˢ.

Bk. 16, *Fo.* 664.

1562.

"I ANN CRYSPE off Marlesford in the counti off Suff w'in the dyocɇ of Norwyche"—"I wyll that my Tenement that I now dwell in called Byrswellɇ wᵗ all the londes that I now have in occvpyenge be leten be my cxecwtors vntyll that Wyllm̃ barrad do cn'the his yerɇ and the mony therof Comyng my howses kepte in good & suffycyent Repracyons I gyve & bequethe to be evenly devyded emonges my foure chyldren that ys to seye John vrsely mergarett and maryon"—"I will that John my sonn shall hauc my Tenement brondɇ wᵗ all the londɇ that I hold by copyc off Court Rolle of the maner of marlesford and Campessye" paying "vnto my three dowghtcrs" £10 apiece—"I will that all my movables stuffe of howshold corne catyll and other movables what so eũ they be be evenly devyded emõgɇ my foure Chyldren"—"Henry Johnson Thoms̃ Wryte & Wyllm̃ barrade" Exᵒʳˢ to each of whom "for ther peynes" 6ˢ 8ᵈ—Witnesses "John sp'ent Thomas Ewyn John Jaffery phyllyp crapenell & others"—Dated 15 Sept 1561—Proved 5 Nov 1562 by Thomas Wrighte & William Barrarde power reserved to the other Exᵒʳ.

Original Will.

1566.

"I NICHOLAS CHRYSPE of donwiche in the countye of Suff Turner"—"to Johane my wiefe my howse that I nowe dwell in with all the appurtenauncɇ therto" for life remʳ equally "to Roberte Cryspe and George Cryspe my two sonnes" with remʳ if they both die without lawful issuc "to Johane and Margeret my two doughters"—"to Johane my doughter" and "to Margeret my doughter" £6 13ˢ 4ᵈ apiece out of said housc &c—"to Johane my wiefe and to her heyres my fenne called the freshe fenne" "kepyng her vnmaryed or els not"—"to Robertc and George my sonnes my two turncs George to have his choysc"—"I will that Georgc shall have his choysc of all my tooles my lyttle shoppe toolcs onelyc excepted takynge but syxe and Roberte to havc the rcste"—"to Gcorge my sonne all my tooles in my lyttle shoppe" —"I will that Jonc my doughtcr shall have a spacc for hyr beddc in the chambcr over the ploure" "dewrynge the tymc she kepeth her vn-

10

maryed "—" to Elyzabeth my doughter the wiefe of Thomas Avye " 40/
—" Jone my wiefe and Thomas Avye my sonne in lawe " Ext˟ & Exᵒʳ to
the latter of whom " for hys paynes " 10/ and said wife resid ʸ Legatee—
Witnesses " Thomas Sewin ffraunce Rychardson and xpofer Belfelde "—
Dated 4 Feb 1566—Proved 6 March 1566-7 by the said Ext˟ & Exᵒʳ.

Bk. 21, Fo. 417.

1569.

" I HENRYE CRISPE of laxfelde in the countye of Suff yeoman "
—" to be buried in the church yarde of Laxfelde aforesayde "—
" vnto Katheren my wiefe and hir assignes all that my tenemente called
Goodwins with all the howses landes " &c to the same for life rem ʳ " vnto
John my sonne and vnto his heyres for ever " paying " vnto Henrye
Crispe his brother " £20—Said son Henry under 21—" vnto Katheryn
my wiefe and John my sonne their executors and assignes the lease of
the tenementes and londes wᶜʰ I do nowe dwell in that I had and took
for certen yeres yet to come of one Nicholas Stanhawe "—" vnto William
Cuñolde my sonninlawe one milche cowe "—" vnto Henrye my sonne
and Susan my daughter eyther of them A good milche cowe "—" Katheren my wiefe and John my sonne " Ext˟ & Exᵒʳ—" Henrye Payne "
Supervisor to whom " for his paynes " 20/—Witnesses " John Moore
Clarke Geffreye Crispe william Stannarde William Haywarde William
Jaye wᵗ others "—Dated 16 April 1569—Proved 23 July 1569 by the
said Exᵒʳ power reserved &c and proved by the said Ext˟ 28 Sept 1569.

Bk. 23, Fo. 32.

1573.

" I ROBT CHRISPE of Busierd in the county of Suff "—" vnto
Wiłłm my Sonne thre milch kine and the chesepresse with the
weighte there vnto belonging " " my Counter table one chaire and a stole
therto " " one hutch with a spring lock and thre paier of Shetes " &c &c
—" vnto Margaret my daughter twoe of the yongest kine and my Cub-
barde my best bedd in the chamber furnished as it is and thre paier of
shetes " &c &c " a silke hatt that was here mothers " &c—" vnto Avis
my Daughter my great black dowde cowe " " two swine one great hogg
and a lesse " &c &c—" vnto Edwarde my Sonne the great long table in
the hall one pewter basen twoe small pewter dishes " " my Carte and
Ploughe with all the Implemente therto belonging " &c &c—" vnto
Edwardes childe my godchild " 5/—" vnto Wiłłm my Sonne and to his
heiers " my houses & lands " in Brusierd Cransforde and Sweftling "—
" Thomas Crispe and John Harding " Exᵒʳˢ—Witnesses " Robt Loñnes
Thomas Collingworth John Harding and others "—Dated 12 Oct 1572
—Proved 10 Dec 1573 by both the Exᵒʳˢ.

Bk. 24, Fo. 448.

1574.

" I THOMAS CRISPE of fframlinghm̄ at the Castell in the county of Suff "—" to be buried In the Church yarde of fframlynghm̄ aforesaid "—" to Elizabeth my wife " my houses orchards & yards in Framlingham for life rem͏ʳ " to georg my Sonne and to theyers of his bodye lawfully begotten "—" to my fouer daughters " viz. " to Katheryn Anne Rose and Alyce " £8 equally between them—" vnto Thomas my sonne and Agnes my Daughter " 4o/—Said wife resid͏ʸ Legatee & sole Ext͏ˣ— Witnesses " Richarde Hugharte Cler̄ and others "—Dated 29 Sept 1573 —Proved 1 Apr 1574 by the said Ext͏ˣ.

Bk. 25, *Fo.* 3.

1576.

" I JOHN CRISPE of Dinington in the countie of Suff and within the Dioces of Norwiche "—" vnto Johan my wief and vnto ffraunces Crispe my son xxiiij deyerye kyne to be pted betwene them "—" to the seid ffraunces my sone all my horses and geldinge Carte carte trase " &c " and my Tumbrells and harrowes "—" to the seid Johan and ffraunces all my brasse and brasen vessell pewter and pewter vessell and all my chese howse stuffe and backhowse stuffe " &c equally between them and they to " occupie my ferme together so longe as it shall please M͏ʳ John Rowse Esquire to suffer them to occupie and haue the same "—" to Anne Crispe my Doughter my thirde posted Bedstede A fetherbed A bolster " &c and £10—" to Symon Crispe my sone tymbre to make hym A bedstede A fetherbed A bolster " &c and £20—" to Christian and Margaret Crispe my Doughters to eyther of them A paire of shetͼ and A pewter platter " and £10—" to M͏ʳ John Rowse Esquire my Landlorde one Angell noble of goulde "—Said wife & son Francis Ext͏ˣ & Ex͏ᵒʳ— Witnesses " Roger Godbolde John Rushe Christopher Hersant Wiħm Woode "—Dated 16 Jan 1575—Proved 11 Apr 1576 by the said Ext͏ˣ & Ex͏ᵒʳ.

Bk. 26, *Fo.* 1.

1576.

" I THOMAS CRISPE of Baddinghm̄ in the county of Suff Carpender "—" to be buried in the churchyard of Baddinghm̄ aforesaied "—" vnto Margaret my wyfe my Messuage or Tenement w͏ᵗʰ all and singuler the landͼ therevnto belonging " in " Sweftlinge in the county of Suff aforesaid " for life but if she marries again then the same " vnto John my sonne " paying " vnto Parnell my Daughter and his sister " 4o/ " vnto Alyce my Daughter " 4o/ " vnto wiħm my Sonne " 4o/ & " vnto ffraunce my Sonne " 4o/—If said son John dies before enjoying the house & lands then the same to said son William he paying the legacies to his sisters and if he dies &c the same to said son Francis and if he also dies &c then the same to said daughters Alice & Parnell equally—" vnto John my sonne aforesaied all that my lond holden by Indenture of the mannoʳ of Brusiarde " " twoe milch kyne " &c—" vnto Parnell my Daughter other twoe like milch kyne " &c—" vnto Alyce my Daughter also other twoe good milch kyne " &c—" vnto wiħm and

12

ffraunçe my sonnes fouer good milch kyne " &c—Said wife resid' Legatee
& she & said son John Ext* & Ex°'—Witnesses " Robt Holland Nicholas
Storke Willm ffolkard and Thomas Smithe wth others "—Dated 23 Jan
1575-6—Proved 4 Sept 1576 by the said Ext* & Ex°'.

Bk. 26, Fo. 101.

1577.

" I WILLM CRISPE of Wayngford in the countye of Suff yeoman "—
" vnto my Sonne Mathewe my Tencment called Barlyebread with
all the landç therto belonginge both fre and coppye and all my other
coppy holde landç wch I have in possession or in remainder to him and
to his heyres for euer and I doe ordaine and make him the sayed
Matthewe my only Executo' "—Dated 27 Jan 1574-5 — Witnesses
" John Smythe and Nicholas Cawson and Willm Bridgeman "—Proved
21 June 1577—Amount of Inventory £24 14^s o^d.

Bk. 26, Fo. 248.

1580.

" I JOHANE CRISPE wedowe of Dunnington in the countie of Suff
and within the dioce of Norwich "—" vnto Margaret Crispe my
daughter my best gowne one plaine bedstead and one flock bedd and
one bolster and fyve powndes "—" vnto Symon Crispe my sonne other
five powndes " " and one deyrie Cowe "—" to Robte Moore and Margerie west one wenned calf "—" ffraunçe Crispe my sonne " resid'
Legatee & sole Ex°'—Witnesses " xpofer hersant and James Moore "—
Dated 14 Dec 1580—Proved 14 Jan 1580-1 by the said Ex°'.

Bk. 28, Fo. 194.

1581.

NUNCUPATIVE Will of " Robte Crispe of Walpole in the countie
of Suff "—" to be buried in the churchyarde of Walpole aforesaied "
—" vnto Johane his wief all and singuler his goodes moueables rightes
credites and Cattalles whatsoeuer desiring her to bringe vpp his children
in the feare of god willing her alsoe to take all suche debtes as were at
the time of his death or after due vnto him vz of Godfrye Crispe of
fresingfilde Tanner fower powndes " " and of Roper Mylles gen't of
Bramefild xxviij^s " &c—Said wife sole Ext*—Witnesses " Thomas Elmer
Daniel Daldy of Starston and Edwarde Browne "—Dated 16 May 1581
—Proved 28 July 1581 by the said Ext*.

Bk. 28, Fo. 343.

1581.

" I ANNE CRISPE of Dunw^ch in the county of Suff wedowe "—" to
be buried in the churcheyarde of St Peters "—" to Sara my Daughter
the fetherbedd that I nowe lye on wth twoe fether traunsomes one

covering of Dornickes one payer of shetes and one playne bedstedd" " one brasse pott with a bayle and twoe brasse keatles vnbownde" &c &c " at the daie of her marriage "—" to Johane Spenser my daughters childe twoe pewter dishes at the daie of *his* marriage "—" my Daughter Mary Trewfote" resid⁷ Legatee & sole Ext˟—Witnesses " M͏ͬ wiᵗᵗm Bulbroke M͏ͬ wiᵗᵗm Sergeant John Jurdyn and Jeffery Wood with others "—Dated 28 July 1581—Proved 28 Sept 1581 by the said Ext˟.

Bk. 28, *Fo.* 410.

1583.

NUNCUPATIVE Will " of Edmund Chrispe of Laxefeld in the countie of Suff Yeoman "—" vnto Roger Calver his sonne in lawe one fetherbed and bolster and all other thinge belonging to the sayd bed and all his apparrell "—" vnto Margaret Calver Dawghter of the sayd Roger one Joyned Cheste "—" All the rest of his goodes howsehould stuff and Implementᵉ of howsehoulde" to be divided equally into four parts one part whereof " he did will and geve amongest the Children of the sayd Roger " the second part " vnto the Children of Agnes ffyske his Dawghter and John Alldred sonne of Robert Aldred" the third part " vnto the Children of Alice Rowe his Dawghter " and the fourth part " vnto the Children of Wiᵗᵗm Jaye his sonne in lawe "—" the foresayd Roger Calver" sole Ex˚ʳ—Witnesses " Jeffrie Chryspe and Thomas Jordon "—Dated 18 March 1582-3—Proved 17 July 1583 by the said Ex˚ʳ.

Bk. 29, *Fo.* 411.

1584.

" I THOMAS CHRISPE of Brusyard in the countie of Suff Carpenter "—" Thomazine Taylor " to " sell my apparrell and devide the monie amongst my brothers and sisters children "—" to Jane Lonnes " 2/—" to Katherine Lonnes" 2/—The said Thomasin resid⁷ Legatee & sole Ext˟—Dated 29 Jan 1584—Adm˚ⁿ with the Will annexed granted 17 Feb 1584-5 to James Chrispe the brother of the deceased the said Thomasin Taylor having renounced.

Bk. 30, *Fo.* 287.

1585.

NUNCUPATIVE Will of " Robert Chrispe of Parham in the countie of Suff and Dioces of Norwich "—" to be buried in the churchyard of Parham aforesaide "—" to Robert Chrispe his sonne two able mylch keene " when 21—" to Thomas Chrispe his sonne two able milch keene " at the same age—" vnto Margaret Chrispe his daugh͏ͭ two able mylch keene " at the same age—" Alice his wyef" resid Legatee & sole Ext˟— Witnesses " Edmund Jordon John Corbold and others "—Dated March 1585—Proved 13 Oct 1585 by the said Ext˟.

Bk. 30, *Fo.* 517.

1589.

" I XP̃AN CRISPE of Reydon in the Covntie of Suff and in the diocese of Norwich "—" vnto Thomas Ayelm̃ my Nephew " 20/ " one pewter platter and a paier of shetes "—" vnto Thomazine ffisuñ " 10/ " one paier of shetes and one pewter platter "—" vnto ffaith Chapman " 10/ " one paier of shetes my best pewter platter "—" I give xp̃ian Crispe my Goddaughter " 6ˢ 8ᵈ " and one Course paier of shetes "— " vnto Marie Dawdie wieff of Daniell Dawdie my Godson one featherbed wᵗʰ the transum "—" vnto the Children of the said Marie " 6ˢ 8ᵈ— " vnto xp̃ian Bales the wieff of ffraunces Bales " 6ˢ 8ᵈ and " one payer of Course shetes "—" vnto ffaith Chapman my bed wheron I lie with all thinges therto belonginge "—" vnto the pore people " of Reydon 3ˢ 4ᵈ— " vnto the pore people " of Waulpoole 3ˢ 4ᵈ—" John Chapman and ffaith his wieff " residʸ Legatees—" Rychard Ayelmer my Brother And John Chapman " Exᵒʳˢ to each of whom 20/ " for ther paynes "—Witnesses " George Chapman and George Harp "—Dated 24 July 1589—Proved 5 Aug 1589 by John Chapman power reserved to Richard Aylemer.

Bk. 32, *Fo.* 402.

1591.

" I HENRYE CRISP of Beccles in the countye of Suff Singlem̃ "— " to my brother Thomas crisp " £3—" to my Sister ffeltum " 20/ " to the goodwife coulman " 22/—" I owe to the goodm̃ Goodinge " 10/ and the said debt " to be payd out of the ffirst monye that shalbe receyued "—" I fforgiue my brother Thomas crisp " 40/—The residue of my goods to be equally divided " betwen my brothers and sisters children viz " " Dorithe vslye and Ann crisp ffrance Antony John charity and Amy charby " and " William crisp Thomas crisp John crispe Edmunde crisp and margaret crisp " and the shares to be paid to them when 21— " my Brother Thomas crisp " sole Exᵒʳ—" Mr. vtting pson of Weston " Supervisor—Witnesses " Thomas Wilson John Domison "—Dated 26 June 1591—Proved 29 Jan. 1591-2 by the said Exᵒʳ.

Bk. 33, *Fo.* 420.

1593.

" I RICHARD CRESP of Parham in the County of Suff and within the dioces of Norwich "—" to be buried in the pish Church yard of Parham aforesaid "—To Annes [called Anne and Agnes elsewhere in the Will] " my wife my Tenement in Parham aforesaid with all and singuler the p'messes and lande thereto belonginge And by me late purchased " for life remʳ " vnto my sonne John and to the heires of his body lawfully begotten " with remʳ to " my daughter Jane " " and to the heires of hir body " &c—" vnto Annes my wife all my moveable goodᵉ " for life and after her decease the same to be equally divided " betwene my said sonne and my daughter "—" vnto my sonne John my best seled bedsted which I lye in with the best ffetherbed and boulster and two fustian pillowes " &c &c and when 22 £5—" Annes my wife and my sonne John Cresp "

15

Ext^x & Ex^{or}—Witnesses "Thomas Harsome and ffraunce Norman "—
Dated 30 Apr 1593—Proved 17 Aug 1593 by the said Ext^x & Ex^{or}.

Bk. 34, *Fo.* 530.

1604.

" I THOM̄S CRISPE thelder of Laxfield in the county of Suff yeo-
man & wthin the Dyoces of Norw^{ch} "—To be " buryed in the Church
yard of Laxfield aforesd "—To "Anne my welbeloved wife" £4 a year
for life and £6 a year more or "her meat drincke and bording for her
self & her mayde " in my messuage or tenement "wherein I doe now
inhabit " &c—"vnto Thom̄s Crisp my sonne his Exe̊ " &c the £40
" menc̄ōned & expressed in one bond or wrighting obligatory" dated 26
Sept 1598 "wherein & whereby one John Crisp late deceassed & Thom̄s
his sonne did stand & are become ioyntly & seū̊ally bounden vnto the
said Thom̄s my sonne for the paym̄ thereof "—"vnto Sampson Crisp
sonne of Nicholas Crisp late deceassed his Exe̊ " &c the £40 men-
c̄ōned & expressed in one bond or wrighting obligatorye" dated 25 July
1601 "wherein & whereby the seid Thom̄s Crisp standeth bounden vnto
the seid Sampson Crisp for the paym̄ " thereof—"vnto John Crisp
Nicholas Crisp Elizabeth Crisp & Anne Crispe the Children of the
seid Thom̄s Crisp my grandchild " £10 apiece—" vnto eū̊y one of my
grandchildren that is to say the children of the seid Thom̄s Crisp my
sonne & of Awdry Cooper my daughter" 40/—"Item I will that after
my deceasse & the deceasse of the seid Anne my wife Elizabeth the late
wife of John Crispe my sonne deceassed shall have " £6 yearly for life
—"vnto Johane the wife of Thom̄s Crisp my grandchild " £10 a year
for life " after the deccasse of the seid Thoms Crisp "—" vnto my
daughter Cowper" 20/ &c "& to eū̊y one of my daughters in law" 20/
—"vnto Margret Pype my goddaughter" 3^s 4^d and "vnto Willm̄ Pype
her sonne and my godsonne " 3^s 4^d—"vnto Thom̄s Lovell Henry Eade
Margret Man Elizabth the daughter of Boune (?) & to John Browne for
whom I have answered as a speciall witnes at Baptisme " 3^s 4^d apiece
when 21—" Thom̄s Crisp my sonne & Willm̄ Cowper my sonne in lawe "
Ex^{ors} & resid^y Legatees—"the seid Anne my wife & my kinsman willm̄
Dowsing" Supervisors to the latter of whom "for his paynes" 10/—
Witnesses "ffrūnce Borret John Borret Thom̄s Brewster Georg Cooper "
—Dated 1 Aug 1601 Codicil dated 1 Aug 1601 & published 28 Feb
1603—Testator speaks therein of having made a Deed of Feoffment to
Robert Borret " Wolfrayne Dowsing" Richard Aldus & " Symon Man "
of all his lands & tenements in Laxfield & other towns adjoining thereto
&c—Witnesses " Georg Coop James Mayes The m̄ke of Christopher los
Thomas Grimsby"—Said Will & Codicil proved 26 Feb 1604-5 by both
the Ex^{ors}.

Bk. 40, *Fo.* 37.

1607.

" I ROGER CRISP of Saxmondhm̄ in the county of Suff husbondman "—"vnto Rob̄t R_uckhm̄ my daughters child " £4 when 20—
"vnto Johane Rackhm̄ my daughters child " £6 when 16—" vnto
Bridget Rackhm̄ " £5 at the same age—The sums so devised to my

daughter's children to be employed to the best use until they attain the said ages "& thone half of the ,pfitt thereof" " vnto Sara Rackhm̄ my daughter now the wife of Roɓt Rackhm̄ & thother half" " to be equallye devyded betwene my sd daughters children "—"vnto ech of my executo˄˄ " 10/—"vnto Avis Booteman my sister " 6ˢ 8ᵈ—"my sd daugh˄ Sara & her sd husband " resid˄ Legatees—"James Crisp my brother & Willm̄ Palm̄ of Saxmondhm̄ " Exᵒ˄ˢ—Witnesses " Nicholas [blank] Alice Saldrone Willm̄ Bucknhm̄ "—Dated 29 Oct 1607—Proved 25 Nov 1607 by James Crisp power reserved to William Palmer.

Bk. 41, *Fo.* 328.

1611.

" I ALICE CRISPE of Thorington in the Cowntie of Suff widdowe " —"vnto Marye *Brome* my daughter one Cowe called Smythe one posted beddsteade seeled standing in the kyching chamber " &c &c— "vnto either of the Children of the saide Marye " viz. " Roɓte & John Broune one yearling heckfer "—" my best cloathe gowne vnto Katheryne ffoxe my syster"—vnto Marye Clarke my sister my blue petticoate my best hatt saving one "—"vnto Richard ffoxe my brother in Lawe the pasturing of his Cowe for one yeare ended at Sᵗ michaell the Archaungell next followinge the date of these ꝑnt℮ " and " the redd hefkers calfe that is weaned this yeare "—" vnto John Broune my sonne in Lawe one quarter of cheese "—vnto Katherine my daughter the ffearm̄ and occupyeing where in I nowe dwell vntil the feast of Sᵗ Mychaell tharchaungell next following the date hereof " &c &c—" vnto John ffeveryeare my brother my Mare my Cheese presse twoo greate Cheese ffatt℮ with the breed℮ belonginge to them two kellers " &c—" my daughters Katherine and Marye " resid˄ Legatees —"the saide Katheryne Cryspe my daughter and John ffeveryeare my brother " Extˣ & Exᵒʳ—Witnesses " Thomas John and Marke Harman Richard ffoxe his m̄ke "—Dated 22 June 1607—Proved 29 June 1611 by the said Extˣ & Exᵒʳ.

Bk. 44, *Fo.* 47.

1614.

" I JEAMES CRISPE of Sᵗ Peters in Southelmham in the County of Suff husbondman "—" to ffynette my wife my tenement Swans with all the Land therto belonging except the Sowth end of the howse of the same tenement called the kitchin and one litle orchyard at the sowthend of the same howse " for life remʳ " to John Crispe my sone and to his heires for ever "—To said son " presently after my decease the kitchin and the Orchyard at the same end before excepted " to whom also " one trundle bed as it standeth on the bedchamber with all the furniture therto belonging and one Coffer "—Said wife resid˄ Legatee & she & said son Extˣ & Exᵒʳ—Witnesses " Richard Arton Nicholas Gooche "—Dated 15 Sept. 1613—Proved 10 May 1614 by Finett the Relict & *James* Crispe the Extˣ & Exᵒʳ.

Bk. 47, *Fo.* 11.

1615.

" I JAMES CRYSPE of Yoxford in the County of Suff and wthin the Dyocesse of Norwich "—"vnto Catherine my wyfe All her Linen and Apparrell to her bodye belonging the vse of one Posted bedsted and the vse of her Bedding and other furniture to the same belonging & vsually occupied wth the same the vse of All other my Lynnen the vse of my Cubbard of two Chestes Three Chayres and allso th̄ vse of. all my Brasse and Pewter whatsoeū during her lyfe "—" to Roḃte Dawson to Margarett Dawson to Anne Dawson & to Briggett Dawson my grande-childrenn " 40/ apiece when 21—"vnto Margaret my daughter the nowe wyfe of Roḃte Dawson my sonne in Lawe " £4—" after my said wyues decease I give to the sayd Margaret my grandechilde the said posteede Bedsteed and all the said ffurniture belonging or vsed to the same " " to my grandechilde Roḃte Dawson " " the Cubbard aforesaid " " to the said Anne my grandechilde one of the said Chestes And to the said Briggett my grandechilde another of my sayde Chestes " and " All my Brasse & pewter shalbee equally devided betweene my said grandechil-dren "—" vnto Roḃte Dawson my sonne in Lawe & his heires for eū All my landes & Teñtẽ whatsoeū And all other my goodẽ Chattells " &c and he sole Ex^{or}—Witnesses " William Larter Margarett Hurrion (?) & Thomas Eade "—Dated 8 Oct 1615—Proved 6 Dec 1615 by the said Ex^{or}.

Bk. 48, *Fo.* 156.

1619.

" I JAMES CRISPE thelder of Aldeburghe in the Covnty of Suff marrynor "—"to bee buried in the Churchyard of S^{ct} Peters in Aldeburghe aforesaid or at the discretion of my executrix heereafter named "—"vnto James Crispe my sonne " 30/ when 21—" vnto Mary Crispe my daughter " 40/ when married—"vnto Alice Crispe my daughter " 20/ at the same time—"vnto Mary Cady my daughter in lawe " 20/ at the same time—"vnto John Barber of Aldeburghe afore-said " 10/ at the same time—" Agnes my wyfe " resid^y Legatee & sole Ext^x—Witnesses " Edward Reynold Beniamyn Dowe & John Cowbridge with others "—Dated 14 Apr 1619—Proved 24 Feb 1619-20 by the said Ext^x.

Bk. 52, *Fo.* 188.

1621.

" I WILLIAM CRISPE of Boyton "—"vnto my sonne William " £10 —"to my daughter Alice " £10—" Annice my wife " resid^y Legatee & sole Ext^x—Witnesses Edward Oliver & Robert Blanchfloure the latter signing by mark—Dated 14 Dec 1621—Proved 17 Jan 1621-2 by *Agnes* the Relict & Ext^x.

Original Will, No. 106.

" I THOM̃S CRISPE of Sibeton in the Countye of Suff husbandman "
—" my Coppihold Tenemcnt holden on the Mannor of Sibeton wᵗʰ
all the landℯ therevnto belonginge wᵗʰ thapp'teññcℯ wᵗʰin one yere after
the decease of Bridget my wyffe to be sould " " by Thoñs Crispe my
sonn " & " Thoñs Sarles my ffyrst wyves sonn " & " the money that that
the sayd Teñte shalbe sould for shalbe evenly pted betwene the sayd
Thoñs Crispe Thoms Sarles & John Crispe my sonn "—" vnto Bridget
my wyffe all suche moveable goodℯ as were her owne before I marryed
wᵗʰ her and those of all the rest of my goodℯ I geve vnto her duringe
the terme of her naturall lyffe "—" the sayd goodℯ after the decease of
Bridget my wyff " equally " betwene the foresayd Thoñs Crispe John
Crispe & Thoñs Sarles "—Said wife sole Extˣ—Witnesses John Harrison (?) & James Durfret "—Dated 10 July 1614—Proved 24 Oct 1622
by the said Extˣ.

Original Will, No. 39, *found in a bundle of Wills labelled*
" *Loose Wills* " *between* 1600 *and* 1700.

1624.

NUNCUPATIVE Will of " William Crispe of Cheddeston in the
countie of Suff yeoman "—" vnto Ann his wife All his goodℯ
Cattells and Chattells whatsoeuer for the paymente of his debtℯ and the
bringinge of his bodie decentlie to the Earthe "—Witnesses James Crispe
& Crispian Crispe—Admᵒⁿ with the Will annexed granted 4 May 1624
to Ann the Relict & universal Legatee.

Original Will, No. 114.

1624.

" I THOMAS CHRISPE of Weston in the county of Suffolke Husbandman "—" unto Margret my wife " £10 and " one milch Cow one
fether bed and other houshold stuffe wᶜʰ my Executor shall thinke con-
venient "—" unto Agnes my daughter the wife of Alexander Johnson " 20/
—" William Bidbanke of Shadingfeild in the sayd county yeoman " sole
Exᵒʳ—Witnesses Thomas Robinson George Bullen Thomas Sherman
Richard Childris & Robert Sone—Dated 26 June 1622—Proved 4 Sept
1624 by the said Exᵒʳ.

Original Will, No. 118.

1625.

" I ANNE CRISPE of Boyton in the Countie of Suff widowe "—
" vnto Raphe Gildersleue my sonne " 40/ and " one flock bed wᵗʰ
all thingℯ belonging thereto "—" vnto Alice ffosdick my daughter two of
my yewes "—" vnto ffrancℯ Stebbing my daughter " 30/—" vnto William
Crispe my sonne " 10/—" vnto Alice Crispe my daughter " 10/—" vnto
Margaret ffosdick my beloved child " 10/ when 15—" Anne Crispe my

daughter" resid^y Legatee & sole Ext^x—" John Knight$_e$ of Capell "
Supervisor to whom 20/—Witnesses " Richard Wellum his marke ffranc$_e$
Crane "—Dated 22 June 1625—Proved 13 Sept 1625 by the said Ext^x.

Bk. 56, Fo. 198.

1626.

N UNCUPATIVE Will of "ffraunc$_e$ Crispe of Sweftling "—" vnto
Thomas Crispe his sonn all his land$_e$ & good$_e$ whatsoe$_ll$ as well
wthin the house as wthout"—Witnesses " Wi**H**m Ewen & Alice Crispe "
—Dated 6 July 1626—Adm^{oa} with the Will annexed granted 31 July
1626 to Thomas Crispe the universal Legatee.

Bk. 57, Fo. 105.

1628.

" I JOHN CRISPE of Sweflinge in the Countie of Suff Carpenter "—
" vnto John Crispe my grantchilde my greate Chist & one little
Coffe standinge by yt in the Chamber I lye " [in] " one box wch is in the
Chamber where Marie Chrisp vse to lye " &c—" vnto Marie Chrisp my
grantchilde the bedstead and bed I doe vse to lye on wth all that is mine
that belonge thervnto as yt standeth & one little Coffe standing by the
bed syde " &c—" all the residue of my good$_e$ wch are now in my said
Chamber where I now lye except one trundle bedsteade wch doe runn
vnder my bed " " vnto the said Mary & John my grantchildren to be
equallie deuided betweene them "—" vnto Elizabeth Chrispe my grantchilde the trundle bedsteade before Excepted " " the bed & boulster w^{ch}
Mary Chrisp widdow my daughter in law doth vse to lie on " &c—
" vnto my Cosen Thomas Chrispe my ioynter wch is vsed wth my
rabbettinge stocke "—" all y^e rest of my tooles & other ymplent$_e$ in the
shopp " " vnto three other of my grantchildren the Children of one
Thomas Arnold to be equallie deuided amongest them "—" I will all my
fire wood shalbe sould & that Marie Chrispe aforesd widdow shall haue "
4/ " of the money therof & the residue I will shalbe deuided betweene
the said John Chrispe Mary & Elizabeth Chrispe my grantchildre͂ "—
" vnto Laurence Pells of Sweflinge aforesd " 10/ and he sole Ex^{or}—Witnesses " Wi**H**m Browne & the marke of wi**H**m Wilson "—Dated 9 Sept
1628—Proved 7 Oct 1628 by the said Ex^{or}.

Bk. 58, Fo. 351.

1629

" I ROBERT CURSPE of Ike in the County of Suffolke weauer "—
" to be buried in the Church yard of ffalstenham in the Countie of
Suff "—" vnto my sonne Wi**H**m all my tooles belongeing to my trade &
occupaco͂n of a weauer & ffyve pownd$_e$ worth of yarne " " one flocke
bedde standing vpon the Chamber wth one Co**H**lett tow sheetes & the
beddstead & boulster "—" vnto Anne my wife one howse freehold or
tenem^t being in Melton in the Countie of Suff " for life rem^r " vnto my
sonne in lawe Thomas Gildersteue & his wife " " giueing *ffyve vnto*

20

John Curspe my grandchild" when 21—"vnto Anne my wife Twentie pownde in money & yf she please pte of it in howsholdstuff"—"my Colt at ffaltenham vnto my sonne Gildersteue his wife "—"vnto Anne my wife the hemp lond in the meadowe & all the ould hempe wch she nowe hath in her Custody "—Said son William to " pte wth one payre of Coomes vnto myne ap$ntice my executo^r payeing him for them Tenne shillinge"—" I giue [my] best Cloake vnto my sonne Wiłłm "—"vnto my grandchild an ould huch & twoe sheetes wch are in the howse wch was the huch & sheetes of Prudence wife of my sonne Roƀt "—Said wife & son-in-law Thomas Gildersteue Ext^x & Ex^{or}—Witnesses " John Harte John Browne his ḿke "—Dated 29 May 1629—Proved 22 June 1629 by the said Ex^{or} the Ex^{ix} having renounced.

Bk. 59, Fo. 2.

1631.

" I JOHN CHRISPE of Marlesford in the Countye of Suff and w^{th}in the diocesse of Norw^{ch} brickstriker "—" my house and tenement Called and knowen by the name of goodcheape wth all the lande therevnto belonging " "in Glemham pva in the Countye aforesayd wch at this p̃sent tyme is nowe morgaged and set oƀ to one Wiłłm Seger of Ipsw^{ch} singlemã for the payment of" £32 . 8 . o to be sold—"vnto Amye my youngest daughter" £10 when 21 out of the money arising by the sale of the said house &c and the residue thereof after payment of my debts to be "equally devided betwine John Chrispe my sonne and Martha my daughter "—" my implemente of househould stuffe being but very feawe I will shall be sould towarde the Charge of my funerall " —" John Bridge of litle Glemham my brother in lawe and Anne Hooker of Mãlesford singlewomã " Ex^{or} & Ext^x—" Daniell Pottle of Glemham aforesd yeamã " Supervisor—Witnesses James Pottle Thomas Stannard —Dated 21 March 1630—Proved last of March 1631.

Original Will, No. 212.

1632.

" I MARY CRISPE of ffresingfeld in the county of Suff widowe and w^{th}in the diocesse of Norw^{ch} "—" vnto James Brame my father a peece of gold of tenne shillinge and to the two daughters of James Brame my brother to either of them a peece of gold of twenty shillinge wch said thre peeces of gold are in thande of my sister in lawe the wyfe of the said James Brame my brother "—" vnto Mary Meene servant to Godfrey Crispe my sonne my best wastcoate & a kerchiffe "—"vnto Mary Berdwell my goddaughter a payer of sheetes & my best ruffe and to the wyfe of Jeremy Botwright my greene wastcoate and to the wyddowe Lebold my old Cloake and my tawney petticoate and to Grace Lebold my russet petticoate and a corse white apron and to Joane Noyse my tawney wastcoate "—" vnto the wyfe of the said Godfrey Crispe and to Henry Downes my sonne in lawe to either of them a silver spoone "— "the said Godfrey Crispe my sonne " sole Ex^{or} & resid^y Legatee he paying " vnto Mary my daughter the wyfe of the said Henry Downes " 20/ a year during her life—"vnto the said Mary my daughter my carsie

21

gowne my little red petticoate my densier carsie petticoate" &c—Witnesses James Brame & Fr. Sancartte (?)—Dated 22 March 1631—Proved 17 April 1632 by the said Ex^or.

Original Will, No. 32.

1637.

" I RICHARD CRISPE of Yoxford in the County of Suff Baker "—
" vnto Margery my wife my house in Yoxfrd aforesd wth the yarde & garden therto adioyning & also all that my brewing & bakeing office wth the vse of all my Vesselle therto belonging & also the vse of all & singuler my moueable goode & all other my psonall estate w^t soeū " for life she " payinge my debtes & kepinge & mayntayninge my children " &c—The house &c after the death of said wife " to my two sonnes Tho : & Richard & their heires for eū " paying " vnto Eliz : my daughter " £50 " vnto Abigaell my daughter " £30 " & vnto Sarah my daughter " £30—" after my sd wiues deceasse my moueable goode & all my psonall estate shalbe equally diuided among all my children then liueing "—Said wife sole Ext^x—" Mr John Bedingfeild " Supervisor to whom " for his care and paynes " £5—Witness Francis Burges—Dated 10 March 1636—Proved 25 Sept 1637.

Original Will, No. 1.

1640.

NUNCUPATIVE Will of " Crispine Crispe late while hee liued of S^ct James in Southelmham in the County of Suff yeoman "—" vnto Elizabeth his wife " for life " the vse of all those goodes and Chattelle wch weere in her possession when hee marryed wth her wch hee bought of Richard Stalham & after hee marryed wth her " and " the vse and pfitt of one heifer "—" vnto James Soane the Sonne of Wiłłm Soane and Crispine Blyndes the sonne of Gyles Blyndes his granchildren and Godsonnes " 40/ when 21—" vnto eū one of his other grandchildren " 20/ " and his will & mynde was either of his sonnes in law should paie the foresaid Legacyes vnto ther owne Children they beinge his executo^rs "—" his two daughters Margarett the wife of Wiłłm Sone and Mary the wife of the said Gyles Blyndes " equal resid^y Legatees—" his two sonnes in law Wiłłm Sone and Gyles Blyndes " Ex^ors—Witnesses George Battele & Samuel Riccard—Dated 17 Feb 1639—Proved 22 April 1640 by both the Ex^ors.

Original Will, No. 32.

1640.

WILL " of Godfrey Crispe of ffresingfeld in the countie of Suff yoman "—" vnto Elizabeth Mary & Alice my daughters All the Messuage or Tenem^t " &c " in Worlingworth in the said county wherin Margaret Brame widowe nowe inhīteth And all the landes " &c " in Worlingworth aforesaid aswell freehold as coppiehold wch the said Margaret doth hold for lyfe " equally between them on the death of the said

Margaret—£600 "together wth the oūplus of this my said last will & testam^t" to be invested in the purchase of freehold or copyhold lands & tenements and the same to said wife for life with rem^r equally to said daughters Elizabeth Mary & Alice—" my Cottage or Tenem^t" &c " in ffressingfeld aforesaid wherin Thomas Shepperd & Henry Downes doe nowe inhīte wth the orchard to the same " to said wife for life for the maintenance &c of said daughters until they attain 21 or marry—" vnto the said Mary my wyfe my posted bedstead in the parlo^r belonging to the Messuage where I now inhīte wth the fetherbed boulster & pillowes " &c—" vnto the said Elizabeth my daughter my cubberd table standing in the hall " " two buffet stooles my second bedsteade " &c &c when 18 or married—" vnto the said Mary my daughter my cubberd table standing in the said parlo^r chamber and two buffet stooles my third bedsteade " &c &c at the same time—" vnto the said Alice my daughter my livery table wth a drawer standing in the said parlo^r & two buffet stooles my fourth bedsteade " &c &c at the same time—" vnto the said Mary my wyfe Elizabeth Mary & Alice my daughters all my brasse & pewter equaly "—" the said Mary my wyfe & John Godbold my brother in lawe " Ext^x & Ex^or—" Symon Godbold my father in lawe & ffrancis Sandcroft " Supervisors—Witnesses James Brame & William Godbold the latter signing by mark—Dated 10 Sept 1640—Proved 27 Feb 1640-1 by the said Ext^x & Ex^or.

Original Will, No. 48.

1645.

" I JAMES CRISPE of Aldeburgh in the County of Suff Boatewright" —" vnto James Crispe my sonne all that pte of my howse and tenem^t wherein I now dwell with the Appurtenançe to the same " and " one fetherbed with the furniture "—" vnto Joane Crispe my wife the other end of my howse with the Appurtenançe wch I lately purchased of Thomas Bucke " for life with rem^r " vnto the Childe that the said Jone Crispe my wife is now withall "—" vnto Christian Chrispe my daughter " £15 " one fetherbed with certayne furniture to the same one Cupboard a Bible a brasse pott and twoe platters "—" vnto Mary Chrisp my Sister " 20/—" the sayd Joane Crispe my wife " resid^y Legatee & sole Ext^x—" Beniamin Wheeler " Supervisor—Witnesses John Denn (?) & Thomas Seaman—Dated 2 Apr 1644—Proved 18 March [or May] 1645 by the said Ext^x.

Original Will, No. 28.

1660.

" I HENERY CRISP of Melton in the County of Suff :"—" vnto my loueing wife Isabell Crisp and to her heires for euer all my houses lands and tenem^ts lyeing and being in Woodbridg in the County aforesd And alsoe all my monyes debts and psonall Estate whatsoeu^r " and she sole Ext^x—Witnesses Edward Stisted & Edward Archar—Dated 15 Oct 1658—Proved 13 Oct 1660 by the said Ext^x.

Original Will, No. 40.

" **I** ISABELL CRESP of melton In the Countey of suffolk wed "—
" vnto Pall Cresp & Jon Cresp & marget Cresp my thre yongest
Cheldren all my mouabell goods that Is to say my housoll stuf money
and lenen and wolen eaquly to be parted betwen them "—" all my howses
& lands " " In wodbredg to my excetors to be sould & the money to be
eaquley parted amonghest all my Cheldren that shall be then leuen "—
" edward Archar of melton my sonne in law " sole Ex^{or}—Witnesses John
Nutell & Susan Smeth both signing by mark—Dated 15 Feb 1659—
Proved 13 Dec 1660 by the said Ex^{or}.

Original Will, No. 41.

" **I** THOMAS CRISP of Kellshall in ye County of Suff Tailor "—" vnto
Elesebeth Cresp my louing wif all my goods mouabls debts bils &
bonds " &c for life after payment of my debts and after her decease the
same " to be equally deuided to my two sons Thomas Crisp & Wiłłm
Crisp shar & shar alike "—" Elizabeth Crisp my louing wif & Thomas
Crisp my Eldest sone " Ext^x & Ex^{or}—Witnesses John Reue & Mary Hunt
the latter signing by mark—Dated 11 May 1661—Proved 8 Oct 1661
by the said Ex^{or} power reserved to the Ext^x.

Original Will, No. 152.

" **I** WILLIAM CRISP of Benhole in the County of Suff husband
man "—" vnto Jane my wife all my mouabal goods with in houses
and with out whatsoeuer towards the bringen vp my Children and for
the payment of all my debts what soeuer "—"vnto my sonne Willam " 10/
—" vnto Cattring my daughter " 10/—" Jane my wif " sole Ext^x—Witnesses John Newson & Robert Trep (?) the latter signing by mark—
Dated 23 Nov 1660—Proved 10 Apr 1662 by the said Ext^x.

Original Will, No. 3.

" **I** PHILLIP CRISPE of Hallesworth in ye County of Suff Blacke-
smyth "—" vnto William Garwood my sonne in Lawe & Alice his
wife All That my Messuage or Tenem^t wth the yards gardens Orchards
and passages to the same " " in Hallesworth aforesd in a street there
called Cheston streete & and nowe in the tenure and Occupacoñ of mee
the sayd Phillip Crispe & the sayd William Garwood " for their lives
rem^r " to the right heire of the sayd Alice for eł " paying " vnto Elizabeth Cobb my daughter " 20/ a year for life—" vnto Elizabeth Cobb my
daughter my house called the Shopp & ye little peece of ground lyeinge
betweene the sayd Shopp in ye streete there called Cheston street " for
life rem^r to " Elizabeth Cobb my grandchild & her heires for eł "—
" vnto my sayd daughter Elizabeth all my workeinge Tooles to the in-

tent she should putt vpp a Chymney in the shopp & make itt a dwellinge house for her selfe & children "—" to Katherine Ramplyn Alice Garwood & Elizabeth Cobb my three daughters all my moveable goods & chattles whatsoeũ not before bequeathed to bee equally pted betweene them (after my funerall chardges & pbate of this my Will shalbee thereout deducted & payd)" paying " vnto Anne Hallocke my eldest daughter or her Assignes " £3—The husbands of said daughters Katherine & Elizabeth living—" the aforesd William Garwood " sole Ex^{or}—" Mr Edmund Wright Attorney att Lawe " Supervisor and " for his paynes I giue him a good payer of Gloves "—Witnesses Dorothy Wright John Nicholls & Thomas Watfeld (?) the said Nicholls signing by mark—Dated 1 March 1658—Proved 20 June 1662 by the said Ex^{or}.

Original Will, No. 57.

1665.

" I JOHN CHRISP of Great Blakenham in the County of Suff wheel-wright "—" to be interred wthin the Church yard of Blakenham Aforesd "—" unto John Lucos my eldest sonn in law " £4—" unto John Lucos my second sonn in law " £4 " and all my working tooles " which £4 " he shall haue and take in timber " " And all ye rest of my timber laid in " " ye sd John Lucos my second sonn in law shall have " " And what ye sd timber shall rise and amount unto over and aboue " £4 " he shall repay to his elder brother John Lucos " &c—" unto Thomas Lucos my youngest sonn in law " £4 when 21 to be taken " in househould goods "—" unto Abigall my loving wife all that my Messuage or tennem^t " with " ye shopps yardes gardens " &c " in Blakenham Aforesd " now in my own occupation for life paying " unto the childe wch she is now wth by me " £20 when 21—Also to said wife " all my moueable goods and Chattles wch are before unbequeathed "—" unto my Aforesd three sonns in law and to Ellinor my daughter in law my Aforesd teñem^t " &c equally between them on the death of said wife " in case ye child wch she is now wth by me doe not liue to Accomplish " 21—Said wife sole Ext^x—Witnesses " Joⁿ ffarlwin " & " John Plumley "—Dated 1 May 1665—Proved 17 June 1665 by the said Ext^x.

Original Will, No. 32.

1667.

" I MARGRETT CRISP of Weselton in ye County of Suffolk widdo " —" unto John Minstrall my sonn in law and to Ann his now wiff " 12^d apiece—" all my bills & bonds and all my goods & Chattels & mouabls whatsoeur unto Elizabeth Crisp my yongest daffter " when 21 and if she dies without lawful issue the same to " be equally deuided Amongst ye Chilldren of John minstrall that Anne his now wiff shall baer him " when 21—" John Buckler & William Storkins " (?) Ex^{ors}—" Robert Hacon " Supervisor—Witnesses " Jonne Grise " & " Margrett Donnett " both signing by marks—Dated 20 Aug 1665—No Act.

Original Wills, 1667, No. 81.

" I RICHARD CRISPE of Framlingham in the County of Suffolke
Tanner "—" vnto Thomas Curtis of Earle Colne in Essex " £30
and he sole Ex^or—" vnto Richard Curtis sonne of the afforesayd
Thomas " £15—" vnto Margret the wife of the sayd Thomas " £5—
" vnto Thomas Curtis son of the sayd Thomas " £3—" vnto Mary Curtis
Daughter of the sayd Thomas " £3—" vnto Thomas Crispe my Brother "
5/—" vnto my sister Susan " £10—" vnto Edward Crispe of Ely my
Nephew " £20—" vnto Margret the wife of Miles Marriot " £3—" vnto
Elizabeth Marriot Daughter of the sayd Miles Marriot " £60 " and more
in Houshold stuffe to the value of " £10—" vnto Christian Batlely of
Grunsborough " 20/—" vnto Elizabeth Blackman " 20/—" But Further
my will and Meaning is that Margrett my wife should haue the use of all
These monies aboue Mentioned during the time of her naturall life "—
Said wife resid^y Legatee—Witnesses Mary Ralph Mary Chambers & John
Dowsing the said Mary Chambers signing by marks—Dated 17 Jan
1667—Proved 7 April 1668.

Original Will, No. 17.

———

1669.

" I ELIZEBETH CRESP of Bardsie in the County of suff wedow "—
" the on half of my goods to my yongest sonne stephen touerds his
bringing of hime vp and the other half of my goods to be equelly devided
betwen my sonne John Cresp and my sonne Josvpe "—" my sonne John
Crespe " sole Ex^or—" my beloued frend Thomas Cossye " Supervisor—
Witnesses " Richard wilby " & " Anne geflings " (?)—Dated 5 Feb 1668
—Proved 3 July 1669.

Original Will, No. 77.

———

1670.

" I MARGARETT CRISPE of fframlingham at the Castle in the
County of Suff widdowe aged and weake in body " &c—" vnto
Henry Easter & Constance Easter my grandchildrin now or late of
Brentwood One striped featherbeed One feather bolster belonging to
that bedd One old Coverlett & one silver spoone to be sould by my
Executrix and equally to be devided betweene them "—" vnto the mother
of Henry Easter & Constance Easter aforesaid my black grogeram
Gowne "—" vnto Christian Simpson the wife of William Simpson of
Grundisburgh my biggest brasse kettle (except one) my middle brasse
skillett " &c—" vnto Elizabeth Vyall of Tottenham high Cross my silke
gowne (if shee be lyveing) "—" vnto Suzan Gowlding one redd vnder
pettycoate & one midlyn pewter platter "—" vnto Elizabeth Marriott my
Grandchilde my brasse bakeing pan my glasse keepe & all the things
that are in it " &c &c—" vnto Prudence Marriott of Bacton my greene
Searge coate "—" vnto John Wells my greate Cofer nowe standinge in
the stable "—" vnto Elizabeth Wells the other Cofer there "—" Margarett
Marriott (the wife of Myles Marriott) my daughter " resid^y Legatee &

sole Ext^x—Witnesses Ann Spalden & Mary Charmbers both signing by marks—Dated 9 May 1669—Proved 15 March 1670-1 by the said Ext^x.

Original Will, No. 140.

1673.

" I THOMAS CRISP of Saxmundham in the County of Suffolke Blacksmith "—" vnto John ffisher my Grandchild all my lands Tenem^{ts} " &c " both free & Coppy lying & being in Yoxford in ye Countie aforesaid " paying " vnto ffaith my welbeloued wife " £4 a year for life and paying after her decease " vnto Mary Milles my daughter now ye wife of Rob̃t Milles of Winkfield in ye Countie aforesaid Wea̋ if she shall happen to surviue ye said ffaith my wife " 40/ a year for life paying also " vnto Mary ffisher & Elizabeth ffisher the two sisters of ye said John ffisher " 10/ apiece yearly for their lives— " vnto ye said Mary ffisher & Elizabeth ffisher " £40 when 21— " vnto Thomas ffisher my grandchild " £20 when of the same age— " vnto John ffisher my grandchild one Table as it stand vpon two frames in ye hall & one forme & one keep one great Chist & one fether bed " &c—" vnto Mary ffisher my grand Child one p^r of sheets two napkines & one pillibere "—" vnto Elizabeth ffisher my grandchild one p^r of sheets two napkines one pillibere one deske & one Cofer "—" vnto Thomas ffisher my Grandchild my steth & Mandrell in ye shope "— " vnto Mary Sarles now ye wife of Richard Sarles of Yoxford in ye Countie of Suff glouer " 20/—" vnto m^r Sam^{ll} Salmon pracher of ye word of God in Saxmundhã aforesaid " 10/—" vnto ffaith my well beloued wife all my Corne & my wood in the yard "—" vnto John ffisher my Grandchild all such rent as shall be dew to me at my decease from Henery Woodard for my lands & tenem^{ts} in Yoxford aforesaid "—" vnto ye Children of " the said " Rob̃t Mills of Winkfield aforesaid y^t are now liueing all ye rest & residue of all my houshold stuffe & implim^{ts} of houshold both lining & wooleing brasse pewter & Iron & all other moueables whatsoeũ as yett vnbequeathed (bills bonds & ready mony excepted) to be equally pted amongest them "—" James Aldus of Saxmundham aforesd drap And ye wthin named John ffisher my grandchild " Ex^{ors} to whom 20/ apiece " for there paynes & trauell "—Witnesses Daniel Jackson Frances Cannon & William Booth—Dated 2 Jan 1671—Proved 3 Dec 1673 by both the Ex^{ors}.

Original Will, No. 35.

1675.

" I ROBERT CRISPE of Letheringham in the County of Suff Taylor "—" All that my messuage or tenement lyeing in Letheringham " " where I nowe live wth all the lands outhouses " &c to be sold " for and towardes the payment of my legacyes "—" vnto Willm Howlett of Crettingham my kinsman " £20—" to Christian Ward of Hoo my kinsman " £20—" vnto ffrances Ward my kinswoman " £5—" vnto Alice Howlett of Winston my sister and her daughter that nowe liveth wth her " £5—" vnto Willm Boyles my kinsman " £20 but my Ex^{ors} to pay out of the same " such debtes as the said Willm Boyles my kinsman

27

shall then owe " and to buy him thereout "a newe suyt of Apparrell wth all other necessaryes therevnto belonging "—"the sonnes & daughters of Alice Howlett my sister and the two daughters of my sister Wards " equal resid^y Legatees—"John Curtis of Woodbridge Hasketon and William Howlett of Crettingham my kinsman " Ex^{ors}—Witnesses "The marke of Witľm Annies (?) John Styred John Bradlaugh"—Dated 25 Aug 1675—Proved 11 Nov 1675 by William Howlet power reserved to the other Ex^{or}.

159 Fauconberge.

1678.

" I LYDIA CRISP of Laxfeild in the County of Suff. Widd."—"unto Ann Crisp my daughter " £10—"unto Mary Crisp and Ann my daughters " £20 apiece when 21—To "my sonne Barnabas " £5—"I give all the overplus money that shall remayne in my supervisors hands more then the abovesaid Legacies and payments following to be equally divided betweene my three daughters Lydia Symonds Mary and Ann Crisp abovesaid " when 21—"Barnabas Symonds my sonne " sole Ex^{or} to whom "for his Care and paines " £5—"Laurence Rous Esqr of Baddingham in the said County" Supervisor—Witnesses "Tho: Sharman Jeffrey Risinge Wm Rye "—Dated 10 June 1676—Proved 11 Oct 1678 by the said Ex^{or}.

37 Edgar.

1684.

" I HENRY CRISPE of Brandiston in the County of Suffolke yeoman "—"vnto Susan Crispe my kinswoman " 20/—"vnto Henry Crispe my kinsman & Godson " 20/ when 7—"vnto Mary my beloved wife All my Goods Cattell & Stocke whatsoever without Doores And all Moueables whatsoever within Doores And All Monies due to mee So long as her naturall life And after the Decease of Mary my loveing wife what shall be left My Will & Minde is That Elizabeth Crispe my Mother And Robert Crispe my Brother shall have & injoy being equally parted between them "—Said wife & brother Robert Ext^x & Ex^{or}—Witnesses "ffinit Tovell Samuel Elm̃rs his Marke Hen : Chapman "—Dated 5 Aug 1684—Proved 16 Sept 1684 by the said Ext^x power reserved to the Ex^{or}.

388 King.

1688.

" I WILL̃M CHRISPE of Bromfield in the County of Suff Linnen weaver "—"vnto James Chrispe the elder of Lingstead pva in the County aforesaid my kinsman & to his heires All my Messuages Landes " &c "in Bramfield aforesaid " "all my wearing appell and Cloathes of what kind soever (my Linnen onely excepted) " and £3—"vnto Witľm Chrispe my kinsman Sonn of the said James Chrispe the Elder & his Heires All my Messuages Landes " &c "in Wissett in the said County" and "all my printed bookes"—"vnto Robert Beart forẗly my Apprentice my Looms my pair of warping barres & the boxes therevnto

28

belonginge " &c " all other my working tools whatsoever belonging vnto my Looms " and 40/—" vnto Elizabeth Brothers my Servant my Chest that stands by the bedstead in the Roome next my shoppe and my Cupboard table standing in the same Roome " &c &c and £3—" vnto my Sister Scott " 20/—" vnto James Chrispe the younger and John Crispe my kinsmen two other of the Sons of the said James Crispe the Elder " £3 apiece—" vnto Alice Garwood of Halseworth aforesaid wid my kinswoman " 40/—" vnto George ffenn of Walpoole Blacksmith & his wife " 20/ apiece—" the said Willm Chrispe my kinsman " sole Exor & residy Legatee he paying " my debts Legacies funerall Expences " &c—Witnesses " Mary Neale Junior Mary Davies Tho: Neale Jo: Newson "—Dated 28 May 1687—Proved 7 Sept 1688 by the said Exor.

363 Prideaux.

1700.

" I ROBERT CHRISP of Shelleigh in ye County of Suff: Yeoman " —" after my debts & funerall charges pd I give & bequeath all my Worldly goods houshold stuff & stock within doors and without unto my daughter Mary Chrisp to her proper use & dispose for ever "—" unto my Sonn Robert " 5/—To " my Sonn Thomas Chrisp " 5/ To " my daughter Olive Wright " 5/—" to my daughter Sarah Chrisp " 5/—" to my grandaughter Alice Wright " 2s 6d—" to my grandchild Robert Chrispe " 2/6—" Mary my daughter " residy Legatee & sole Extx—Witnesses " Robt Martin Robert Martin ffrancis Martin "—Dated 14 May 1698—Proved 6 July 1700 by the said Extx.

56 Clarke.

1705.

" I ISRAEL CRISPE of Beccles in ye County of Suffl Clapboardhewer "—" unto my daughter Mary & her heires my messuage or tenemt wth ye outhouses yards & app'tennces in Beccles " paying " unto Margarett my loving wife " £4 a year for life and if she dies before said wife leaving no lawful issue the said messuage &c " unto my sd wife Margarett & her heires for ever " paying " unto such person or psons as my sd daughter shall appoint " £50—" All my psonall estate I give after my debts & funerall charges satisfyed equally to be divided between my sd wife & daughter "—" my cousin John Crisp of Wrentham " sole Exor —Witnesses " Jacob Crispe Isaac Crispe Jno ffarr "—Dated 6 July 1705 —Proved 2 Oct 1705 by the said Exor.

43 Yallop.

1706.

" I WILLM CRISPE of Aldeburgh in ye County of Suffl: Marriner " —" unto Martha my welbeloved wife all & singuler my houses lands & tenemts wth ye app'tennces thereunto belonging lying & being in Aldeburgh " for life " for & towards ye bringing up of my childrenn wth all & singuler my goods & chattels w'soever " and after her decease the same " to be equally divided between my children " but if she marries again the same "to be & continue unto my children" "iｍediately after her so contracting marriage"—Said wife sole Ext^x—Witnesses "The m^rke of Alexander Styles The m^rke of Richard Reynolds Jeremiah Walker"—Dated 15 Apr 1706—Proved 20 June 1706 by the said Ext^x.

53 Yallop.

1706.

" I EDWARD CRISP of Woodbridge Hasketon in ye County of Suff^1 : Yeoman"—"unto Elisabeth my well beloved Wife all my goods & chattels within doores & wth out after my decease Provided y^t She pay my debts and funerall charges"—"unto John Crisp of Chasfield ye elder" 5/ "to his Sonn John" 5/ "to his Sonn Edward" 10/ "& to all ye rest of his children y^t shall be alive w^thin three months after ye longest Surviv^r of both" 5/ apiece—"Robert Capon in ye Hamblett of All-stones" sole Ex^or "& I doe give unto Robert Capon & Deborah his Wife all ye goods & chattels y^t shall be left by ye longest surviv^r to y^m for ever"—Witnesses "Anne ffowle Joseph Amis"—Dated 20 Nov 1706—Proved 15 March 1706-7 by the said Ex^or.

93 Yallop.

1708.

" I JOHN CRISPE of Wrentham in ye County of Suff^1 : Yeoman"— "to Sam^ll Crispe my brother all those my Messuages lands" &c "in Henstead & Sotterly in ye s^d County of Suff^1" for life rem^r "to Hester his daughter & ye heires of her body lawfully begotten or to be begotten" rem^r "to John Crisp ye Sonn of Nath^ll Crispe & John ye Sonn of Ezra Crispe of Swafeland & to their heires & assignes for ever equally" but "Eliẓ: my loving Wife" to have thereout 30/ a quarter for life—"to Wiℓℓm Crispe of Stoven in ye said County my kinsman all those my Messuages lands" &c "in Reydon & Wangford in ye s^d County" paying "to ye s^d Eliẓ: my Wife" 30/ a quarter for life—"to ye s^d Wiℓℓm Crispe my kinsman" £100 "for & towards ye paym^t of his ffines & other inci-dent charges"—"unto ye s^d Eliẓ: my Wife" £160—"unto Israel Crispe my brother" £20 "unto Israel his eldest Sonn" £10 "to his daught^r Wife of Sam^ll Cotton of Peasenhall Hoopmaker" £5 "to his Sonn Blessed" £10 "to his Sonn Moses" £10 "to his daughter Sarah" £10 "to his Sonn John" £10 "& to his youngest daughter" £10 the legacies to all the said children when 21—"unto Nath^ll Crispe my brother" £20 "to his Sonn Nath^ll" £10 "to his Sonn John" £10 "to his daughter Eliẓ:" £10 "to his daughter Hannah" £10 "& to his daughter Martha" £10 the said legacies to all these children when 21 —"unto Mr Augustine Plumbstead" £5—"to Mr Wilshire of Swafe-land" £5—"all my messuages lands" &c "in Covehith a^ts Northales in ye s^d County of Suff^1 shall be sold" "& ye moneys thereoff arising I will shall be imployed towards ye paym^t of my debts legacys & funerall expences"—"ye s^d Sam^ll Crispe & Wiℓℓm Crispe" equal resid^y Legatees & Ex^ors—Witnesses "Barbary Crispe her m^rke Mary Johnson her m^rke Lau: Deane"—Dated 26 March 1707—Proved 29 May 1708 by both the Ex^ors.

187 Yallop.

"I EZRA CRISPE Sen̄ of Swefling in ye County of Suff Yeoman" —"unto Ann my beloved Wife my Messuages & Lands in Swefling now in ye Occupation of Samuell Jordan late Everetts" for life rem^r "unto John Crispe my Sonn and to y^e heirs of his body lawfully begotten" rem^r "unto Hannah Crispe my daughter and to her heirs for ever"—"I will that y^e Messuage wherein I now Dwell with all and Singular y^e Lands thereto belonging and y^e Messuages & Lands now in y^e Occupation of John Howell in Swefling $afores^d$ shall be sold"—"unto Moses Crispe my son" £50 when 21 but if he dies under that age the same to be equally divided "between Blessett Crispe my Sonn and Sarah Patrick my daughter"—"unto John Crispe my sonn and Hannah Crispe my daughter" £50 apiece when 21—"unto Ezra Crispe my son and to his heirs all my Messuages Lands" &c "in Halesworth in ye S^d County"—"unto ye S^d Ann my Wife" £30 and £20 more towards "ye Maintenance and Education of my two Yongest Children"—"vnto ye S^d Moses Crispe my sonn a silver Tancklar that was his mothers and two silver spons and to Blessett Crispe my sonn" 5/—"and to Sarah Patrick my daughter two silver spoons and to Hanah my daughter a little trunck that was her mothers one silver spoon" &c—"unto Mary Cotten my daughter" £5 "& a little spoon"—"y^e s^d Ezra Moses Blesset and John my sonns Mary Sarah & Hannah my daughters" equal $resid^r$ Legatees —"Samuell Crispe my brother & ffrancis Patrick my sonn in Law" Ex^{ors} to each of whom £5—Witnesses "Mary Mowle" & "Edmond Bass"—Dated 25 Dec 1710—Proved 6 Feb 1710-1 by both the Ex^{ors}.

58 *Raymond.*

1711.

WILL of Thomas Crisp [described in the Calendar as of Orford]— "to my Louing wife Mary Crisp my house & shope and all ye purtenas there belonging During her noteriell Life firder I giue her all my goods & mony to pay my debts"—"I make Mary Crisp my sole exsecter"—Witnesses Thomas Thurston Richard Sweft & John Cobb— Dated 13 Feb 1711—Proved 10 March 1711-2 by the said Ext^x.

Original Will, No. 125.

1712.

"I BARBARAH CRISPE of Wrentham Widow in the County of Suff:"—"unto $Will^m$ Agus my Sisters Son" £30—"unto Anne Agus the daughter of Thomas Agus my Sisters Son" £30—"unto Amarus Ward of Henstead my Kinsman" £10 and if he dies within three months after my decease the same equally "amongst his wife and Children"— "unto Anne Agus aforesaid my best trunk & what I shall leave in it" and she $resid^r$ Legatee but if she dies before receiving her legacy "my Kinsman William Agus shall have" the same—"Benjamin Downing of ffrostenden sole Executor" to whom 40/ "for his trouble and pains"— Witnesses "Jacob Stanton Anne Haylouck Clement Haylouck"—Dated 24 March 1710—Proved 29 March 1712 by the said Ex^{or}.

194 *Raymond.*

" I JAMES CRISPE of Bramfield in the County of Suffolk Yeoman"
—"unto my Son John Crispe of Bulcham in the County of
Suffolk & to his heirs for Ever All my Messuages Lands " &c
"in Bramfield aforesaid "—"unto my Son William Crispe of Bramfield
in the County aforesaid " £50 "All the Overplus money which I shall
leave after the Legacies are paid" and "my Bed & all my household
Goods "—" my will is that all my wearing Cloaths Neckcloaths & Shirts
Shoes & Stockins be Equally parted after my decease between my two
Sons John Crispe aforesaid & William Crispe "—"to my Daughter
Margery the wife of William Hailocke of Bramton in the County of
Suff " £10—"to my daughter Sarah Benefield the wife of John Benefield
the Sume of Ten pounds liveing in *Ba*mfield in the County of Suffolk "
—"to my Daughter Elizabeth Bagett of Linstead in the County of Suff
Widow" £10—"to my Grandchild James Crispe the Son of James
Crispe now dec^d " £5—" my Son William Crispe of Bramfield in the
County of Suffolk " sole Ex^or—Witnesses Nathaniel Copping Anne
Walker & William Dunston the said Anne signing by mark—Dated 24
Nov 1715—Proved 23 March 1715-6 by the said Ex^or.

196 *Sturges.*

" I ELIZABETH CRISPE of Wrentham in the County of Suffolk
widow "—" unto Easter Crispe the wife of Simon Crispe of Wrentham my Sister ". £15—" unto Mary the wife of Mr Isaac Alstone Wool-
comber in Ipswich in the Said County and unto Elizabeth the wife of
Nicholas Wincopp her Sister the two daughters of my brother William
Rix of Wrentham dec^d " 20/ apiece—" unto Sarah the daughter of
Stephen Robinson of Wrentham aforesaid " 40/—" unto John Crispe the
Son of Nathaniel Crispe of Wrentham aforesaid " 40/—" unto Elizabeth
the daughter of Samuel Carver of ffrostenden the interest of twelve pounds
yearly " for life and after her decease " my Exec^r hereafter named Shall
divide the Sume of Twelve pounds equally between the Surviveing
Brothers & Sisters of the s^d Elizabeth Carver "—" unto ·Easter the wife
of Simon Crispe aforesaid my two best Suits of Apparrell & all my wearing Linnen "—" my Kinsman Simon Lyell of Wrentham aforesaid " sole
Ex^or & resid^y Legatee he paying my debts legacies &c but if he dies
without lawful issue then the overplus after his decease and the payment
of said debts &c " unto Easter the wife of Simon Crispe aforesaid
Mary the wife of Isaac Alstone afores^ed Elizabeth the wife of Nicholas
Wincopp & Easter the wife of Stephen Robinson " equally—Witnesses
" Lydia Seamer John Lincolne "—Dated 10 Dec 1718—No Act, but the
previous & the following Wills in the Register were proved in Oct 1719.

106 *Wilkin.*

" I WILLIAM CHRISPE of Bramfield in the County of Suffe Hus-
ban "—" unto my Son William Chrispe All my messuages Lands "
&c in Wissett paying £5 " a year towards the bringing up of my three

youngest children" till they attain 18 and then paying "to my Son James Chrispe" 40/ a year for life—"to my Son James Chrispe" £50 "when my daughter Sarah" attains 18—"to my Son William Chrispe" £50—"to my Son Edward Chrispe" £50 "when my youngest daughter" attains the same age—"unto my Son John Chrispe" £60 "when my youngest daughter" attains 21—"to my three daughters Mary Susan & Sarah" £50 apiece when 24—"All the Overplus I give to Susan my wife" for life but if she marries again "it Shall be divided amongst my Six Children James Edward John Mary Susan & Sarah"—"my Son William Chrispe & Susan my wife" Ex^or & Ext^x—"my brother John Chrispe" Supervisor—"if the s^d Susan my wife do chance to marry again" she "Shall have twenty pounds to dispose of at her will & pleasure"— Witnesses "Sam. White Wm Browne his mark Frances Reinolds her mark" —Dated 30 May 1719—Proved 22 Sept 1719 by the said Ex^or & Ext^x.

93 Wilkin.

1723.

WILL of John Crisp [described in the Calendar as of Bulchamp]— "unto Margrate Crispe my beloved wife All my Lands at Oxford" for life or she to sell the same if she pleases—"unto Margrate my wife All my Lands in Bramfield" for life rem^r "to my Son James and my Son William" equally—"unto my Sons James and William" £15 apiece when 25—"unto my eldest Son John Crispe" 40/ "to be paid yearly at the <i>first</i> of St Michaell"—"unto my Son Everett" £50 when 25—"unto my Son Francis" £50 when 24—"unto my youngest Son Robert" £50 when 22—"to my daughter Mary" £50 when 25—"unto my daughter Ann" £50 when 21—"to my Daughter Margrate" 5/—"unto [my] loving & tender wife All my Goods & chattles to <i>the</i> bring up my Family" and she sole Ext^x—"Mr William Maggs of Halesworth" Supervisor to whom "for his Trouble" £5—Witnesses "John Wiggett John Haylouck Eliz. Huet her ꝑke"—Dated 18 Feb 1720-1—Proved 29 Nov 1723 by the said Ext^x.

399 Wilkin.

1723.

"I MARY CRISP of Oreford in the County of Suffolk"—"First I will that my Debts & funerall charges Shall be paid and discharged and what remain after they are paid & discharged I give to Edward Riggs Son of my Daughter Mary Riggs to be by her laid out for him to the best advantage towards binding him out to a Trade"—"I will that my wearing Cloaths & Linnen be equally divided between my three Daughters"—"to my Daughters Margaret & Rebecca" 5/ apiece—"my Daughter Mary Riggs" sole Ext^x—Witnesses "Geo: Kerridge The mark of Eliz: Garrard"—Dated 15 Jan 1723—Proved 11 March 1723-4 by the said Ext^x.

416 Wilkin.

f

" I ROBERT CHRISP of Wrentham in the County of Suffolk Cooper "—" unto Elizabeth my loveing wife my Tenement wherein I now dwell and also my other Tenement in Wrentham in the occupation of Zadoc Wilkerson with the Appurteñces thereto belonging " for life rem^r of the former " unto Ann Crispe my daughter " and of the latter " unto Elizabeth Crispe my Youngest daughter "—" unto John Crispe my son " 5/—" unto Mr William Crispe of Wrentham my Kinsman and Executor hereafter named " £3—" unto Elizabeth Crispe my daughter one silver Cupp and two silver spoons and unto Ann Crispe my daughter four silver spoons "—The residue of my Personal Estate after payment of my debts legacies &c to said wife for life and after her decease the same to " my two daughters " equally—" my loveing Wife Elizabeth and Mr William Crispe aforesaid " Ext^x & Ex^{or}—Witnesses " Samuell Morses John Lincolne John Girling Juner "—Dated 2 Feb 1724—Proved 23 Oct 1725 by the said Ext^x & Ex^{or}.

71 *Bishop.*

1726.

" I MARGARET CRISP of Bulham in the County of Suffolk widow " —" my will & mind is that all my Lands in Melton & Ufford or in any other Town adjacent in the County of Suffolk be Sold " " And the money ariseing therefrom to be paid to my Children as herein after mençoned "—" unto my eldest Son John " £20—" unto William my Son " £5—" unto James my Son " £5—" unto Robert my Son " £40 —" unto ffrancis my Son " £20—" unto Edward my Son " £20—" unto Sarah my eldest daughter " £10—" unto Mary my Daughter " £30— " unto Ann my youngest daughter " £50 when 21—" my will & mind further is that when the Land be Sold that if it amounts to more than the Suñes before menconed that it Should be divided between my Said children Share & Share alike "—" all my Lands in Orford or in any other Town adjacent in the County of Suffolk " to be let or employed " for the best advantage for my eldest Son John And after the disbursement of Taxes " &c " the Overplus to be paid to him my Said Son half yearly for the time of his naturall life & after his decease to be equally divided between my s^d children which Shall be then liveing "—" Everard Woods of Westleton in the County of Suffolk Gen't " sole Ex^{or}—Witnesses " Elizabeth Aldiss John Blanden Ann Wade her mark "—Dated 17 Aug 1726—Proved 18 Nov 1726 by the said Ex^{or}.

154 *Bishop.*

1729.

WILL of " Nathaniell Chrisp of Wrentham in the County of Suff " —" unto Elizabeth my wife and Executrix hereafter named All my Goods Chattells Cattell " &c " and other my personall Estate of what Nature or kind soever for & towards the payment of my Debts Funerall Charges " &c " & the Overpluss I give unto her my said wife " for life and " such & so much of my personall Estate as shall be & remain at the decease of my said wife shall be equally divided between all mine and her Children (viz) Nathaniell & John Chrisp Elizabeth the wife of William Reeve Hannah and Martha Chrisp William and James Johnson or so many of them as shall be then living but my mind and will is that William Johnson who have had Eight pounds paid him in the time of my Life should have that Eight pounds accounted in his part And also that Elizabeth the wife of William Reeve who have had in my Life time the Value of Forty Shillings should have that Forty Shillings accounted in her part of the Overpluss "—Witnesses " John Lincolne Philip Barker" —Dated 6 Jan 1714—Proved 24 Nov 1729 by the said Ext*.

175 Tanner.

1385419

1732.

" I SIMON CRISPE of Wrentham in the County of Suff Yeoman "— " unto Easter my Loving wife All my Messuage Lands " &c " in Henstead in the s^d County " for life rem^r "unto William Crispe my Son & his heirs for Ever "—" unto Sarah Crispe my youngest Daughter All those my Messuages Lands" &c " in Sotterton in the said County " when 21 to her also " So much out of my Stock and Personal Estate as Shall be necessary to answer the Purchase of that third part of the Estate in Soterton to which I am not as yet intituled and also So much more out of my Stock and personal Estate as Shall be necessary to Satisfy the Expences of my daughter Sarah's Admission to the Copyhold Lands belonging to my Estate in Sotterton And that other *other* third part which I have not as yet purchased "—" unto William Crispe my Son all my wearing Apparrel and wearing Linnen "—" Easter my Loving wife " & " Mr John Lincolne of Wrentham " Ext^x & Ex^{or} & the former resid^y Legatee—Witnesses " John Rix James Sayer The mark of Martha Browne "—Dated 6 March 1731—Proved 1 Apr 1732 by John Lincolne, power reserved &c.

366 Tanner.

1736.

" I JOHN CRISPE of Marlesford in the County of Suffolk Yeoman " —" unto my Son Thomas Crispe of Clopton " £5—" unto my Son Samuel Crispe of Sternfield " £5—" when all my Debts and funerall Charges be paid my Will is that all my stock and money that is good should be fairely aprized and the money arising thereby should be equally parted to my Seven Children or to their heirs " and " whereas there is fifty Pounds and Eight Years Interest due at Lady day next from Mr Sowes of Knatshall due upon Bond and when that money be paid My Will is that it shall be parted equaly to my Seven Children or their heirs "—" my Son Thomas Crispe of Clopton and my Son Samuel Crispe of Starnfield " Ex^{ors}—Witnesses " Edward Reeve Anne Reeve Elizabeth York "—Dated 12 Feb 1735-6—No Act, but entered in the Calendar under the year 1736.

186 Leman.

" I WILLIAM CRISPE of ffrostenden in the County of Suffolke
Yeoman "—"unto John Crispe of Wangford in the County aforesaid my Son and to his Heires for ever All those my Messuages lands
Tenements and Appurtenances both ffreehold and Copyhold scituate
lyeing and being in Wangford and Raydon in the said County and now
in the occupation of the said John Crispe" paying " unto William Crispe
of Wrentham my Eldest son " £50—"unto Samuel Crispe my Youngest
son and unto his heires for ever all those my Messuages Lands " &c
"both freehold & Copyhold " " in ffrostenden aforesaid " paying " unto
William Crispe of Wrentham my Eldest son " £150—Said son William
sole Ex^or & resid^y Legatee—Witnesses Mary Carman William Reeve &
John Lincoln the said Mary & William signing by marks—Dated 27 June
1740—Proved 26 Aug 1740 by the said Ex^or—Inventory under £20.

Original Will, No. 16.

1748.

" I SUSANNAH CRISP of Bramfield in the County of Suffolk
Widow "—To be " Interred in the Church Yard of Bramfeild
Aforesaid "—" To Mary Kindred my Daughter " £50—" To Susannah
Banks my Daughter " £50 and " my Smallest Chest now in my posses-
sion "—" to Sarah Holmes my Daughter one Guinea "—Also to said
children equally " all my household linnen and wearing Apparrell both
Linnen and Woollen "—" to James Crisp my Son " £55—" to Jams
Crisp my Grandson the son of Jams Crisp my Bed that I now lye on "
—" to Edward Crisp my Son my House and all the Land " &c " thereto
belonging lying and being in Rendham in the County aforesaid " and
£5—" to my Son John Crisp " £50—" Jams Crisp and John Crisp my
Sons " Ex^ors & resid^y Legatees—Witnesses " John Coppinge Eliz Coppinge Thos Randall "—Dated 20 Oct 1747—Jurat of the said James
Crisp 5 Dec 1748, power reserved to John Crisp the other Ex^or.

Fo. 91.

1750.

" I JOHN CRISP of Becles in the County of Suffolk Gentleman "—
" unto Hannah my beloved Wife and to her heirs and Assigns for
ever All my real Estate of what nature or kind soever " and she to " sell
dispose of and Convert such part and so much of my household Goods
ffurniture and other my personal Estate of what Nature or kind soever
as will be sufficient to pay and Satisfy all my just Debts which I shall
owe at my decease ffuneral Charges and the Charge of the probate of
this my Will "—The residue of said Personal Estate to said wife and she
sole Ext^x—Witnesses " Osm^d Clarke Isaac Lincoln William Corner "
—Dated 19 Jan 1748—Jurat of the said Ext^x 26 Nov 1750.

P. 224.

1754.

" I ROBERT CRISP of Ipswich in the County of Suffolk Innkeeper"
—"to my Father John Crisp and Hannah his Wife" £5 apiece—
"to my Brother John Crisp" £5—"to my Sister Elizabeth Keynon"
£5—"to my Brother in Law George Ablett" £5—"my loving Wife
Elizabeth Crisp" resid^y Legatee & she & "Mr John Ellis of Ipswich
aforesaid Inn Keeper" Ext^x & Ex^{or}—Witnesses "And^w Baldry W^m
Keeble"—Dated 25 Oct 1752—Jurat of the said Ext^x & Ex^{or} 21 Oct
1754.

Fo. 136.

1777.

" I SAMUEL CRISPE of ffrostenden in the County of Suffolke Yeoman"—"unto Hannah my loving Wife All my Messuages Lands"
&c "in ffrostenden aforesaid" for life to her also "the use of all my
Stock & moveables so long as she" "shall choose to continue in the
Occupation of my said Lands" "maintaineing & Educateing all my
Children and paying the yearly Interest of such Sum or Sums as I shall
owe at the Time of my decease but if my said Wife Hannah shall choose
to depart from the Occupation of my said Lands in ffrostenden or
shall think proper to marry againe" my Ext^x & Ex^{or} shall "sell off all
my stock & moveables Except so many of my Household Goods as
shall be fairly valued at" £15 "which Goods I give to my said Wife"
and they "shall pay off my just Debts"—After the death of said wife
" All my Messuages Lands and Tenements in ffrostenden aforesaid shall
be sold" £50 shall be paid out of the money thus arising "unto William
my Son" and the residue thereof shall be equally divided "between my
Son William and all my other Children" when they attain 21—"my
loving Wife Hannah Executrix and William Crispe of Wrentham my
Brother Executor"—Witnesses "Ja^s Oliver Simon Rix John Lincoln"—
Dated 24 Jan 1754—Jurat of the said Ext^x & Ex^{or} 25 Feb 1777.

Fo. 16.

1781.

" I JOHN CRISP of Wangford in the County of Suffolk Merchant"
—"unto Steffe Crisp my Youngest Son" my messuage or tenement in Wangford wherein I now dwell with the malting office & the
houses lands &c thereto in Wangford or parishes adjoining "as well
ffreehold and Charterhold as Copyhold" &c but " Martha my dear and
loving Wife and Thomas Crisp (one other of my Sons) together with
the said Steffe Crisp" to hold & occupy the same "for their joint and
equal benefit" &c for 5 years from the 10th of Oct next after my decease
the said Steffe receiving rent during the said term "as owner or Pro-
prietor of the said Estate"—"to the said Martha my Wife such of
my Household Goods and ffurniture as she shall make choice of not ex-
ceeding" £30 in value and a legacy of £800—"unto Samuel Crisp my
eldest Son" £600—"unto James Crisp John Crisp and William Crisp
my Sons" £600 apiece—"to the said Steffe Crisp my Son" £150

37

twelve months after my decease or when he attains 21—£800 to be invested for the benefit "of the said Thomas Crisp my Son" for his life & on his decease the said sum equally "unto the said Samuel Crisp James Crisp John Crisp William Crisp and Steffe Crisp my Sons and to Martha Crisp my Daughter"—"to the said Martha Crisp my Daughter" £100—£500 to be invested for the benefit of said daughter Martha for her life for her own separate use & benefit "notwithstanding any Coverture she shall happen to be under" and after her decease the said sum to be paid to such person or persons as she shall appoint by her Will &c—Testator held a farm in Wangford or parishes adjoining thereto from Sir John Rouse Barᵗ—Residue of Personal Estate equally to said wife Martha & children Samuel Thomas James John William Steffe & Martha—"the said Samuel Crisp my Son and Peter Jermyn of Halesworth in the said County of Suffolk Gentleman" Exᵒʳˢ to the latter of whom £5 "for his Care and Trouble"—Witnesses "H. Newson John Wright Jnᵒ Tuthill"—Dated 8 Aug 1777—Jurat of both the Exᵒʳˢ 7 June 1781.

Fo. 61.

1783.

WILL of "Robert Crisp of Wickham Market in the County of Suffolk Labourer"—"I will and order that all my just Debts ffuneral Charges and Testamentary Expences shall be fully paid and satisfied And after payment thereof I give and bequeath all the rest of my Goods Chattles and Personal Estate to my Daughter Elizabeth Mays and I do hereby nominate and appoint Warner Litsenburg of Petistree in the said County ffarmer sole Executor of this my Will"—Witnesses "Simon Paternoster Robᵗ Minter"—Dated 20 May 1783—Jurat of the said Exᵒʳ 22 July 1783.

Fo. 84.

1786.

WILL of "Samuel Crisp of Great Glemham in the County of Suffolk Farmer"—"my Brothers Thomas Crisp and Robert Crisp" Exᵒʳˢ to whom £25 apiece—"to my Nephews Richard Manthorp and Samuel Manthorp" £30 apiece when 21—"to my Nephew Samuel Plant" £30 when of the same age—The residue of my Personal Estate after payment of my debts &c to be equally divided between "my Brother John Crisp" "my said Brother Thomas Crisp" "my said Brother Robert Crisp" "my Sister Sarah the Wife of Cornelius Beddingfield" "my Sister Susanna the Wife of Richard Wilkinson" "my Sister Hannah the Wife of Edmund Plant" & "my Sister Elizabeth the Wife of John Heffer" —Witnesses "The Mark of Milicent Emmons Simon Paternoster"— Dated 21 Apr 1785—Codicil dated 22 Nov 1785—The legacies bequeathed to said nephews Richard Manthorp & Samuel Manthorp to be increased to £50 apiece and to be paid to them when 21—Witnesses "The Mark of Alice Rackham Simon Paternoster"—Jurat of both the Exᵒʳˢ 16 March 1786.

Fo. 24.

WILL of " John Crisp of Bramfield in the County of Suffolk Farmer" —" Ann my beloved Wife sole Executrix"—My messuage or tenement with the wheelwright's shop &c "in Bruisyard in the said County " in the occupation of James Smith & his under-tenants & my messuage or tenement with the hemp land thereto by estimation 1 acre in the occupation of Samuel Ife his assigns &c " in Rendham in the said County " to be sold & my debts to be paid out of the money thus arising & out of the rents of the said premises until sold the overplus of the said money together with the residue of my Personal Estate to said wife for life—My messuage or dwelling house divided into 3 tenements with the outhouses &c in Bramfield in the occupation of William Smith James Smith & Knights Bedingfield or their assigns & my messuage or dwelling house divided into 2 tenements with the orchards &c in Bramfield in the occupation of John Eade & Samuel Smith to said wife for life— Ann Rayner late wife of Jonathan Rayner of Bramfield farmer by her Will dated 16 May 1775 gave to Testator's said wife by the name of Ann Crisp her daughter her copyhold messuage in Halesworth in the said county with the outhouses &c thereto now in the occupation of John Hatcher grocer for life with rem^r to Ann Crisp her grandchild Testator's daughter her heirs &c & Testator & his said wife having surrendered the premises sometime since to the said John Hatcher he gives to his said daughter after his wife's decease the messuage &c in Bramfield in the occupation of the said John Eade & Samuel Smith on condition that she when 21 surrenders & releases to the said John Hatcher all her estate right &c to the said premises in Halesworth—After the decease of said wife the messuage &c in Bramfield in the occupation of the said William Smith James Smith & Knights Bedingfield to be sold and the money thus arising with the rents of the said premises until sold & the residue of my Personal Estate then remaining to said daughter Ann & John & William Crisp my two sons equally but the value of the said messuage &c in the occupation of John Eade & Samuel Smith to be deducted from said daughter's share—Witnesses " John Woods John Eastaugh Will Hatcher "—Dated 1 Dec 1787—Jurat of the said Ext^x 4 March 1788.

Fo. 16.

1792.

WILL of "Moses Crisp of Easton in the County of Suffolk Innholder "—" to my Daughter Maria Aldrich " my cottages &c in Easton aforesaid in the occupation of Robert Hayward chairmaker Thomas Grimwood tailor & William Edwards gardener—" to Mary my beloved Wife " my messuage tenement or inn with the land &c to the same in Easton in my own occupation for life rem^r " to my Son Moses Crisp his heirs " &c—My Personal Estate to be appraised but " no account shall be taken of any particular pieces of old Gold or Money in my said wife's possession used as pocket pieces or kept for antiquity sake " of " my wearing Apparel of all sorts " which I give to said son Moses or of " such things as belonged to Mary my wife at the time of her intermarriage with me " which I give to said wife—After payment of my debts funeral charges &c £100 out of my said Personal Estate to be invested for the benefit of said wife for life and after her decease £50 of this amount to said daughter and the remaining £50 to said son—To "my brother Samuel Crisp" £5 out of my said Personal Estate & the residue thereof to my said daughter & son—"my Son in Law Robert Aldrich and my Brother in Law Stephen Catchpole" Ex^ors—Witnesses "Charles Garrard Charles Beard Simon Paternoster"—Dated 9 July 1789—Codicil dated 30 Jan 1790—"Whereas I have declined publick Business and am removed out of my Inn called the white Horse into an apartment or Cottage belonging to those mentioned in my within written Will which are therein given and devised to my Daughter Maria Aldrich" notwithstanding such gift "Mary my beloved wife shall have her dwelling and residence in the apartment wherein she my said Wife and I now dwell for and during the Term of her natural Life without paying any Rent for the same"—Also to said wife for life "the use and Occupation of all and singular my Household Goods and Furniture of in and belonging to the said Apartment" and after her decease the same equally to said son & daughter—Witnesses William Edwards Margaret Edwards & Simon Paternoster the said Margaret signing by mark—Jurat of both the Ex^ors 5 July 1792.

Fo. 68.

1799.

"I EDWARD CRISP of Yoxford in the County of Suffolk Farmer" —After payment of my just debts & funeral charges "all my Moneys Goods Chattels" &c whatsoever "to Sarah Crisp my dearly beloved Wife" for life and after her decease the same equally "between John Crisp my only beloved Son and Sarah Haward Wife of Char^s Haward of Flixton in the said County my well beloved Daughter"— Said son John & Charles Haward Ex^ors—Witnesses "Jabez Cole Wm Stammers Jn° Eastaugh"—Dated 18 Feb 1793—Jurat of both the Ex^ors 18 May 1799—Effects under £100.

Fo. 50.

Administrations.

8

Administrations.

1610-1. 2 March Adm^{on} to THOMAS CRISPE late of Wingfilde dec^d granted to Agnes the Relict Robert Goodwin joining in the Bond. The said Agnes sworn 21 Feb 1610-1.

Act Book No. 1, Fo. 23.

1612. 2 July Adm^{on} to JAMES CRISPE late of Bramfilde dec^d granted to Alora [in Latin] the Relict.

Act Book No. 1, Fo. 61.

1613. 29 June Adm^{on} to ROBERT CRISPE late of Rumburghe dec^d granted to Anne the Relict.

Unbound & Unnumbered Act Book, Fo. 94.

1618-9. 16 Feb Adm^{on} to MARTHA CRISPE late of Snape dec^d granted to John Crispe the Son.

Act Book No. 4, Fo. 48.

1623-4. 6 Jan Adm^{on} to JOHN CRISPE late of Bedfilde dec^d granted to Theophila Crispe the Sister Henry Cushen (?) joining in the Bond.

Act Book No. 6, Fo. 22.

1631. 24 Nov Adm^{on} to WILLIAM CRISPE late of Cheddesten dec^d granted to Katherine Wiett alias Crispe Wife of Francis Wiett of Snape the Relict the said Francis joining in the Bond.

Act Book No. 10, Fo. 22.

1639. 3 May Adm^{on} to THOMAS CRISPE late of Donwich dec^d granted to John Crispe of Beccles the Maternal Uncle [Avunculus] during the minority of Elizabeth Crispe the Daughter.

Act Book No. 17, P. 14.

1640. 3 Nov Adm^{on} to THOMAS CRISPE late of Hallisworth dec^d granted to Margaret the Relict.

Act Book No. 18, *P.* 49.

1642. 9 July Adm^{on} to WILLIAM CRISPE late of North Coue dec^d granted to Ann the Relict " Jo Cooke " joining in the Bond.

Act Book No. 20.

1642. 10 Dec Adm^{on} to ANN CRISPE late of North Coaue dec^d granted to Thomas Crispe the Father of William Crispe late the Husband John Staffer joining in the Bond.

Act Book No. 20.

1663. July 31 Adm^{on} to HENRY CRISPE late of Kelshall dec^d granted to Mary the Relict William Ewing of Middleton Yeoman joining in the Bond.

Act Book No. 22, & *Bundle of Bonds endorsed* 1663.

1664. Bond of £200 dated 19 May from Penelope Crispe of Hallisworth co. Suffolk Widow & Thomas Scarlett of the same Yeoman [but the latter's name crossed through] for the Adm^{on} of the Goods &c. of JOHN CRISPE late of Hallisworthe dec^d by the said Penelope his Relict.

Bundle of Bonds at the Archdeacon's Office labelled 1663-69.

1677. 14 Dec Adm^{on} to ROSE CRISPE late of Walberswicke dec^d granted to William Gilding the Son John Benefire [or Benefote] of Dunwich Gent. joining in the Bond of £100.

Act Book No. 30.

1677-8. 9 March Adm^{on} to THOMAS CRISPE late of Raydon dec^d granted to Margaret Westgate alias Crispe the principal Creditor.

Adm^{on} Register 1673-1708, *Fo.* 21.

1680. 24 April Adm^{on} to WILLIAM CHRISPE late of Blithburgh dec^d granted to Mary Chrispe the Relict.

Act Book No. 34.

1683. 19 May Adm^{on} to ROBERT CRISPE late of Wrentham dec^d granted to Elizabeth Crispe the Relict.

Adm^{on} Register 1673-1708, *Fo.* 53.

1687. 20 May Adm^{on} to RICHARD CRISPE late of Darsham dec^d granted to Mary Crispe Widow the Relict William Aldred of Darsham joining in the Bond of £100.

Act Book 1684-88.

1687-8.   28 Feb Adm^{on} to ABRAHAM CRISPE late of Gorlston dec^d granted to Thomas Crispe the Paternal Uncle & Guardian of Susan, Abraham, & Mary Crispe, minors, the Children, Thomas Pope of Gorlston joining in the Bond of £400.

Act Book 1684-88.

1689-90.   13 March Adm^{on} to ROBERT CRISPE late of Brandeston dec^d granted to Elizabeth Crispe Widow the Relict Bartholomew Crispe of Bredfeild & John Earle of Framlingham joining in the Bond of £200.

Act Book 1688-93.

1693.   13 Dec Adm^{on} to ROBERT CRISPE late of Beccles dec^d granted to Richard Bendy the principal Creditor William Crisp of Beccles joining in the Bond of £20.

Act Book No. 40.

1695.   28 Nov Adm^{on} to THOMAS CRISPE late of Hollesworth but dying in the King's service in the ship " Restauracon " granted to Susan [or Susanna] Crispe the Mother.

Act Book No. 40.

1699-1700.   19 Jan Adm^{on} to THOMAS CRISPE late of Westleton but dying in the ship " Suffolke " granted to Mary the Relict.

Act Book No. 40.

1709.   Bond of £120 dated 13 Oct from Alexander Crispe of Theberton co. Suffolk Yeoman Stephen Lane of Middleton in the said co. Yeoman & Peter King of Hallesworth in the same co. Yeoman for the Adm^{on} of the Goods &c of ALEXANDER CRISPE late of Knattishall dec^d by the above Alexander his Son.

Adm^{on} Bonds 1708-11, *No.* 88.

1720.   Bond of £200 dated 30 Apr from John Chrisp of Snape co. Suffolk Yeoman John Paruman of the same & John Doe also of the same for the Adm^{on} of the Goods &c of ISAAC CHRISP late of Snape dec^d by the said John Chrisp his eldest Son.

Adm^{on} Bonds endorsed 1716-19, *No.* 175.

1722.   Bond of £80 dated 21 Nov from Mary Chrispe of Woodbridge co. Suffolk Widow James Swan of Ufford in the said co. & Stephen Brightwell of Woodbridge in the same co. for the Adm^{on} of the Goods &c of THOMAS CHRISP late of Woodbridge by the said Mary his Relict.

Adm^{on} Bonds 1720-22, *No.* 168.

1733-4. Bond of £200 dated 2 March from Stephen Robinson of Wrentham co. Suffolk Grocer & William Bobbet of North Cove in the said co. Yeoman for the Adm^{on} of the Goods &c of SAMUEL CRISPE of South Cove lately dec^d by the said Stephen Robinson & Esther his Wife who was the only Daughter of the said dec^d.

Adm^{on} Bonds 1731-34, *No.* 130.

1736. Bond of £200 dated 17 Dec from Mary Crispe of Bramfield co. Suffolk Widow & George Browne of Sibton in the said co. Yeoman for the Adm^{on} of the Goods &c of WILLIAM CRISPE late of Bramfield dec^d by the said Mary Crispe. Inventory £169 . 10^s . 0^d.

Adm^{on} Bonds 1734-36, *No.* 144.

1755. Bond of £100 dated 1 May from Margaret Crispe of Aldeburgh co. Suffolk Widow for the Adm^{on} of the Goods &c of THOMAS CRISPE the younger late of Aldeburgh intestate dec^d by the said Margaret his Relict.

Adm^{on} Bonds 1751-55, *No.* 122.

1778. Bond of £40 dated 3 Apr from Lydia Cripps of St Peter's in Ipswich co. Suffolk Widow for the Adm^{on} of the Goods &c of WILLIAM CRIPPS late of the same parish intestate dec^d by the said Lydia his Relict.

Adm^{on} Bonds 1778, *No.* 12.

1789. Bond of £100 dated 5 May from Joseph Penney of Aldeburgh co. Suffolk Baker Thomas Starkweather of the same Perukemaker & William Schuldham of Carlton in the said co. for the Adm^{on} of the Goods &c of ELIZABETH CRISP late of Aldeburgh Widow intestate dec^d by the said Joseph her Cousin & next of kin.

Adm^{on} Bonds 1789-90, *No.* 10.

1789. Bond of £400 dated 14 July from James Crisp of Bramfield co. Suffolk John Crisp of Halesworth in the said co. & James Hanton also of Halesworth for the Adm^{on} of the Goods &c of MARY CRISP late of Bramfield Spinster & an Orphan intestate dec^d by the said James Crisp her Brother.

Adm^{on} Bonds 1789-90, *No.* 34.

1798. Bond of £100 dated 29 June from William Crisp of Beccles co. Suffolk Soapboiler Joseph Austin of the same Gent. & George William Browne Bohun also of the same Gent. for the Adm^{on} of the Goods &c of MARTHA CRISP late of Southwold in the said co. Widow intestate dec^d by the said William Crisp her Son.

Adm^{on} Bonds 1797-98, *No.* 46.

Index.

INDEX OF NAMES.

Chapman, Faith, 15 ; George, 15 ; Henry, 28 ; John, 15.
Charby, Amy, 15; Anthony, 15; Charity, 15; Francis, 15; John, 15.
Childris, Richard, 19.
Chitting, William, 3.
Churchman, John, 5.
Clarke, Mary, 17 ; Osmond, 36.
Clover, John, 7.
Cobb, Elizabeth, 24, 25 ; John, 31.
Cole, Jabez, 40.
Coleman, —, 15.
Collingworth, Thomas, 11.
Cooke, John, 44.
Copping, Elizabeth, 36 ; John, 36 ; Nathaniel, 32.
Corbold, John, 14.
Corner, William, 36.
Cossy, Thomas, 26.
Cotton, Mary, 31 ; Samuel, 30.
Cowbridge, John, 18.
Cowper, or Cooper, Audrey, 16 ; George, 8, 16 ; John, 7, 8, 10 ; William, 16.
Crane, Francis, 20.
Crapenell, Philip, 10.
Cresy, John, 7.
Cripps, Lydia, 46 ; William, 46.
Crispe, Abigail, 22, 25 ; Abraham, 45 ; Agnes, Annes, or Annice, 3, 6, 7, 12, 14, 15, 18, 19, 43 ; Alexander, 45 ; Alice, 5, 6, 8, 9, 12, 14, 17-20, 22-25, 27, 28 ; Alora, 43 ; Amy, 21 ; Andrew, 4 ; Annabel, 3 ; Anne, 7-10, 12, 13, 15, 16, 19-21, 25, 28, 31, 33, 34, 39, 43, 44 ; Audrey, 16 ; Avis, 11, 17 ; Barbara, 30, 31 ; Bartholomew, 45 ; Blessed, or Blessett, 30, 31 ; Bridget, 19 ; Christian, 4, 8, 12, 15, 23 ; Clemens, 6 ; Crispian, 19 ; Crispine, 22 ; Dorothy, 15 ; Easter, Esther, or Hester, 30, 32, 35, 46 ; Edmund, 5, 8, 14, 15 ; Edward, 11, 26, 30, 33, 34, 36, 40 ; Elizabeth, 6, 9, 11, 12, 16, 20, 22-26, 28, 30, 32, 34, 35, 37, 38, 43-46 ; Everett, 33 ; Ezra, 30, 31 ; Faith, 27 ; Finette, 17 ; Frances, 8 ; Francis, 12, 13, 20, 33, 34 ; George, 10, 12 ; Godfrey, 13, 21, 22 ; Hannah, 30, 31, 35-38 ; Henry, 6, 7, 11, 15, 23, 28, 44 ; Isaac, 29, 45 ; Isabel. 23, 24 ; Israel, 29, 30 ; Jacob, 29 ; James, 14, 17-19, 23, 28, 29, 32-34, 36-38, 43, 46 ; Jane, 15, 24 ; Jeffrey, 6, 7, 11, 14 ; Joane, 3, 4, 7-14, 16, 23, 24 ; John, 3-8, 10-13, 15-17, 19-21, 24-26, 29-40, 43-46 ; Joseph, 26 ; Katherine, 5, 11, 12, 17, 18, 24, 25, 43 ; Lydia, 28, 46 ; Margaret, 6-15, 18, 19, 22, 24-26, 29, 33, 34, 44, 46 ; Margery, 3, 8, 9, 22, 32 ; Maria, 39 ; Marion, 5, 6, 10 ; Martha, 21, 29, 30, 35, 37, 38, 43, 46 ; Mary, 14, 17, 18, 20-23, 27-29, 31, 33, 34, 36, 39, 40, 44-46 ; Matthew, 13 ; Moses, 30, 31, 39 ; Nathaniel, 30, 32, 34, 35 ; Nicholas, 10, 16 ; Olive, 29 ; Parnell, 12 ; Paul, 24 ; Penelope, 44 ;

Crispe—*continued.*
Philip, 24 ; Prudence, 21 ; Pryme, 9 ; Rebecca, 33 ; Richard, 15, 22, 26, 44 ; Robert, 4-6, 9-11, 13, 14, 20, 21, 27-29, 33, 34, 37, 38, 43-45 ; Roger, 16 ; Rose, 9, 12, 44 ; Sampson, 16 ; Samuel, 30, 31, 35-38, 40, 46 ; Sarah, 13, 17, 22, 29-36, 38, 40 ; Simon, 6, 7, 12, 13, 32, 35 ; Steffe, 37, 38 ; Stephen, 26 ; Susan, or Susanna, 11, 26, 28, 33, 36, 38, 45 ; Theophila, 43 ; Thomas, 4, 5, 7, 8, 11, 12, 14-16, 19, 20, 22, 24, 26, 27, 29, 31, 35, 37, 38, 43-46 ; Ursula, 10, 15 ; William, 3-6, 8, 11-13, 15, 18-21, 24, 28-30, 32-39, 43-46.
Cunnold, William, 11.
Curspe, Anne, 20, 21 ; John, 21 ; Prudence, 21 ; Robert, 20, 21 ; William, 20, 21.
Curtis, John, 28 ; Margaret, 26 ; Mary, 26 ; Richard, 26 ; Thomas, 26.
Cushen, Henry, 43.

D.

Daldy, Daniel, 13, 15 ; Mary, 15.
Davies, Mary, 29.
Dawling, Jeffrey, 6 ; Robert, 10.
Dawson, Anne, 18 ; Bridget, 18 ; Margaret, 18 ; Robert, 18.
Deane, Laurence, 30.
Denn, John, 23.
Doe, John, 45.
Domison, John, 15.
Donnett, Margaret, 25.
Dowe, Benjamin, 18.
Downes, Henry, 21, 23 ; Mary, 21.
Downing, Benjamin, 31.
Dowsing, John, 26 ; William, 16 ; Wolfrayne, 16.
Dowsing, *alias* Smythe, John, 3.
Dunston, William, 32.
Durfret, James, 19.

E.

Eade, Henry, 16 ; John, 39 ; Thomas, 18.
Earle, John, 45.
Eastaugh, John, 39, 40.
Easter, Constance, 26 ; Henry, 26.
Edmund, Thomas, 7.
Edwards, Margaret, 40 ; William, 39, 40.
Ellis, John, 37.
Elmer, Samuel, 28 ; Thomas, 13.
Emme, 5.
Emmons, Milicent, 38.
Eve, *alias* Sparhawke, Elizabeth, 7.
Everett, —, 31.
Ewing, Thomas, 10 ; William, 20, 44.

F.

Farlwin, John, 25.
Farr, John, 29.
Feltum, —, 15.
Fenn, George, 29.
Ferrore, William, 8.
Feveryeare, Alice, 17 ; John, 17.
Fisher, Elizabeth, 27 ; John, 27 ; Mary, 27 ; Richard, 4 ; Thomas, 27.
Fiske, Agnes, 9, 14 ; Hester, 9 ; Jeffrey, 8 ; Joane, 8-10 ; John, 8, 9 ; Margaret, 8-10 ; Nicholas, 8-10 ; Robert, 6 ; William, 8, 9.
Fisun, Thomasine, 15.
Folkard, William, 13.
Fosdick, Alice, 19 ; Anne, 19 ; Margaret, 19.
Fowle, Anne, 30.
Foxe, Katherine, 17 ; Richard, 17.

G.

Garrard, Charles, 40 ; Elizabeth, 33.
Garwood, Alice, 24, 25, 29 ; William, 24, 25.
Gildersleve, or Gildersteve, Anne, 19 ; Ralph, 19 ; Thomas, 20, 21.
Gilding, William, 44.
Girling, John, 34.
Godbold, or Godbald, Anne, 9 ; John, 8, 9, 23 ; Mary, 23 ; Roger, 8, 12 ; Simon, 23 ; Thomas, 9 ; William, 23.
Golding, Susan, 26.
Gooche, Nicholas, 17.
Gooding, —, 15.
Goodwin, Robert, 43.
Goreham, Geoffrey, 4.
Grigg, Thomas, 6.
Grimsby, Thomas, 16.
Grimwood, Thomas, 39.
Grise, Joane, 25.

H.

Hacon, Robert, 25.
Hanton, James, 46.
Harding, John, 11.
Harman, John, 17 ; Mark, 17 ; Thomas, 17.
Harp, George, 15.
Harrison, John, 19.
Harsome, Thomas, 16.
Harte, John, 21.
Harvy, Robert, 5.
Hatcher, John, 39 ; William, 39.
Haylock, Anne, 25, 31 ; Clement, 31 ; John, 33 ; Margery, 32 ; William, 32.
Hayward, Charles, 40 ; John, 40 ; Robert, 39 ; Sarah, 40 ; William, 11.
Heffer, Elizabeth, 38 ; John, 38.
Hersant, Christopher, 12, 13 ; John, 8.
Holland, Robert, 13.
Holmes, Sarah, 36.
Hooker, Anne, 21.

Howell, John, 31.
Howlett, Alice, 27, 28 ; William, 27, 28.
Huet, Elizabeth, 33.
Hughart, Richard, 12.
Hunt, Mary, 24.
Hurrion, Margaret, 18.

I.

Ife, Samuel, 39.

J.

Jackson, Daniel, 27.
Jacob, John, 4.
Jaye, William, 11, 14.
Jeffery, John, 10.
Jenning, Roger, 7.
Jennings, Anne, 26.
Jermyn, Peter, 38.
Johnson, Agnes, 19 ; Alexander, 19 ; Henry, 10 ; James, 35 ; Mary, 30 ; William, 35.
Jordan, or Jurden, Edmond, 14 ; John, 3, 14 ; Samuel, 31 ; Thomas, 14.

K.

Keeble, William, 37.
Kent, Anne, 7 ; Edward, 7 ; John, 7.
Kerridge, George, 33.
Keynon, Elizabeth, 37.
Kindred, Mary, 36.
King, Peter, 45 ; William, 8.
Knight, John, 20.
Kyrspe, Alice, 5 ; Edmund, 5 ; John, 5 ; Marion, 5 ; Robert, 5 ; Thomas, 5 ; William, 5.

L.

Lane, Robert, 10 ; Stephen, 45.
Larter, William, 18.
Lebold, Grace, 21.
Leche, John Kyrspe, 6.
Lincoln, Isaac, 36 ; John, 32, 34-37.
Litsenburg, Warner, 38.
Lonnes, Jane, 14 ; Katherine, 14 ; Robert, 11.
Los, Christopher, 16.
Love, or Lowe, Robert, 9.
Lovell, Thomas, 16.
Lucos, Eleanor, 25 ; John, 25 ; Thomas, 25.
Lyell, Simon, 32.

M.

Maggs, William, 33.
Man, Margaret, 16 ; Simon, 16.
Manne, Robert, 8.

51

Manthorp, Richard, 38 ; Samuel, 38.
Marriott, Elizabeth, 26 ; Margaret, 26 ;
  Miles, 26 ; Prudence, 26.
Martin, Francis, 29 ; Robert, 29.
Mason, Nicholas, 6.
Mayhew, Alice, 8, 9 ; Audrey, 8 ; John,
  8, 10.
Mays, Elizabeth, 38 ; James, 16.
Meene, Mary, 21.
Miles, or Mills, Mary, 27 ; Robert, 27 ;
  Roper, 13.
Minstrall, Anne, 25 ; John, 25.
Minter, Robert, 38.
Moore, James, 13 ; John, 11 ; Robert,
  13.
Morses, Samuel, 34.
Mowle, Mary, 31.

N.

Neale, Mary, 29 ; Thomas, 29.
Newson, H., 38 ; John, 24, 29.
Nicholas, Simon, 7.
Nicholasson, Robert, 4.
Nicholls, John, 25.
Noloth, John, 4.
Norman, Francis, 16.
Noyse, Anne, 8-10 ; Joane, 21 ; John,
  8-10 ; Martha, 9 ; Thomasine, 9.
Nutell, John, 24.

O.

Oliver, Edward, 18 ; James, 37.

P.

Palmer, William, 17.
Paruman, John, 45.
Paternoster, Simon, 38, 40.
Patrick, Francis, 31 ; Sarah, 31.
Payne, Henry, 11.
Paynter, —, 8.
Peers, Alexander, 4 ; —, 8.
Pells, Laurence, 20.
Penney, Joseph, 46.
Petit, Joane, 4.
Plant, Edmund, 38 ; Hannah, 38 ; Samuel,
  38.
Plumley, John, 25.
Plumpton, Anne, 8-10 ; Thomas, 8, 9.
Plumstead, Augustine, 30.
Pole, Robert, 9.
Pope, Thomas, 45.
Pottle, Daniel, 21 ; James, 21.
Pype, Jeffrey, 7 ; Margaret, 7, 16 ;
  Thomas, 7, 8 ; William, 7, 16.

R.

Rackham, Alice, 38 ; Bridget, 16 ; Joane,
  16 ; Robert, 16, 17 ; Sarah, 17.

Ralph, Mary, 26.
Ramplin, Katherine, 25.
Randall, Thomas, 36.
Rayner, Ann, 39 ; Jonathan, 39.
Reeve, Anne, 35 ; Edward, 35 ; Eliza-
  beth, 35 ; John, 24 ; William, 35, 36.
Reynold, Edward, 18.
Reynolds, Frances, 33 ; Richard, 30.
Riccard, Samuel, 22.
Richardson, Francis, 11.
Riggs, or Rix, Edward, 33 ; Elizabeth,
  32 ; John, 35 ; Mary, 32, 33 ; Simon,
  37 ; William, 32.
Rising, Jeffrey, 28.
Robinson, Easter, or Esther, 32, 46 ;
  Sarah, 32 ; Stephen, 32, 46 ; Thomas,
  19.
Rouse, Sir John, 38 ; John, 12 ; Lau-
  rence, 28.
Rowe, Alice, 14.
Rushe, John, 12.
Rye, William, 28.

S.

Saldrone, Alice, 17.
Salmon, Samuel, 27.
Sancartte, Fr., 22.
Sandcroft, Francis, 23.
Sarles, Mary, 27 ; Richard, 27 ; Thomas,
  19.
Sayer, James, 35.
Scarlett, Thomas, 44.
Schuldham, William, 46.
Scott, —, 29.
Seaman, Thomas, 23.
Seamer, Lydia, 32.
Seger, William, 21.
Sergeant, William, 14.
Sewin, Thomas, 11.
Sharman, Thomas, 28.
Shepperd, Thomas, 23.
Sherman, Thomas, 19.
Simpson, Christian, 26 ; William, 26.
Smith, or Smythe, Alice, 8 ; Godfrey,
  8 ; James, 39 ; John, 5, 6, 10, 13 ;
  Nicholas, 4 ; Roger, 8 ; Samuel, 39 ;
  Susan, 24 ; Thomas, 13 ; William, 4,
  39.
Smythe, *alias* Dowsing, John, 3.
Soane, James, 22 ; Margaret, 22 ; Robert,
  19 ; William, 22.
Sowes, —, 35.
Spalding, Ann, 27.
Sparhawke, *alias* Eve, Elizabeth, 7.
Spearman, Thomas, 17.
Spenser, Joane, 14.
Sprent, John, 10.
Staffer, John, 44.
Stalham, Richard, 22.
Stammers, William, 40.
Stanhawe, Nicholas, 11.
Stannard, Anne, 10 ; Nicholas, 8 ;
  Thomas, 21 ; William, 11.
Stanton, Jacob, 31.